MURDER
BY
CANDLELIGHT

MURDER BY CANDLELIGHT

TEN CLASSIC CRIME STORIES FOR WINTER

Edited by Cecily Gayford

Catherine Aird · Carter Dickson
Cyril Hare · J. S. Fletcher
Dorothy L. Sayers · Fergus Hume
Ethel Lina White · Freeman Wills Crofts
Sapper · Simon Brett

Profile Books

First published in Great Britain in 2024 by
PROFILE BOOKS LTD
29 Cloth Fair
London EC1A 7JQ
www.profilebooks.com

1 3 5 7 9 10 8 6 4 2

Typeset in Fournier by MacGuru Ltd
Printed and bound in Great Britain by
CPI Group (UK) Ltd, Croydon CR0 4YY

A CIP catalogue record for this book is available from the British Library.

ISBN 978 1 80522 255 2
eISBN 978 1 80522 256 9

Contents

Gold, Frankincense and Murder

Catherine Aird

'Christmas!' said Henry Tyler. 'Bah!'

'And we're expecting you on Christmas Eve as usual,' went on his sister Wendy placidly.

'But ...' He was speaking down the telephone from London, 'but, Wen ...'

'Now it's no use your pretending to be Ebenezer Scrooge in disguise, Henry.'

'Humbug,' exclaimed Henry more firmly.

'Nonsense,' declared his sister, quite unmoved. 'You enjoy Christmas just as much as the children. You know you do.'

'Ah, but this year I may just have to stay on in London over the holiday ...' Henry Tyler spent his working days – and, in these troubled times, quite a lot of his working nights as well – at the Foreign Office in Whitehall.

What he was doing now to his sister would have been

immediately recognised in ambassadorial circles as 'testing the reaction'. In the lower echelons of his department it was known more simply as 'flying a kite'. Whatever you called it, Henry Tyler was an expert.

'And it's no use your saying there's trouble in the Baltic either,' countered Wendy Witherington warmly.

'Actually,' said Henry, 'it's the Balkans which are giving us a bit of a headache just now.'

'The children would never forgive you if you weren't there,' said Wendy, playing a trump card; although it wasn't really necessary. She knew that nothing short of an international crisis would keep Henry away from her home in the little market town of Berebury in the heart of rural Calleshire at Christmastime. The trouble was that these days international crises were not nearly so rare as they used to be.

'Ah, the children,' said their doting uncle. 'And what is it that they want Father Christmas to bring this year?'

'Edward wants a model railway engine for his set.'

'Does he indeed?'

'A Hornby LMS red engine called *Princess Elizabeth*,' said Wendy Witherington readily. 'It's a 4-6-2.'

Henry made a note, marvelling that his sister, who seemed totally unable to differentiate between the Baltic and the Balkans – and quite probably the Balearics as well – had the details of a child's model train absolutely at her fingertips.

'And Jennifer?' he asked.

Wendy sighed. 'The Good Ship Lollipop. Oh, and when you come, Henry, you'd better be able to explain to her how it is that while she could see Shirley Temple at the pictures – we took her last week – Shirley Temple couldn't see her.'

Henry, who had devoted a great deal of time in the last ten days trying to explain to a Minister in His Majesty's Government exactly what Monsieur Pierre Laval might have in mind for the best future of France, said he would do his best.

'Who else will be staying, Wen?'

'Our old friends Peter and Dora Watkins – you remember them, don't you?'

'He's something in the bank, isn't he?' said Henry.

'Nearly a manager,' replied Wendy. 'Then there'll be Tom's old Uncle George.'

'I hope,' groaned Henry, 'that your barometer's up to it. It had a hard time last year.' Tom's Uncle George had been a renowned maker of scientific instruments in his day. 'He's nearly tapped it to death.'

Wendy's mind was still on her house guests. 'Oh, and there'll be two refugees.'

'Two refugees?' Henry frowned, even though he was alone in his room at the Foreign Office. They were beginning to be very careful about some refugees.

'Yes, the rector has asked us each to invite two refugees from the camp on the Calleford Road to stay for Christmas this year. You remember our Mr Wallis, don't you, Henry?'

'Long sermons?' hazarded Henry.

'Then you do remember him,' said Wendy without irony. 'Well, he's arranged it all through some church organisation. We've got to be very kind to them because they've lost everything.'

'Give them useful presents, you mean,' said Henry, decoding this last without difficulty.

'Warm socks and scarves and things,' agreed Wendy

Witherington vaguely. 'And then we've got some people coming to dinner here on Christmas Eve.'

'Oh, yes?'

'Our doctor and his wife. Friar's their name. She's a bit heavy in the hand but he's quite good company. And,' said Wendy drawing breath, 'our new next-door neighbours – they're called Steele – are coming too. He bought the pharmacy in the square last summer. We don't know them very well – I think he married one of his assistants – but it seemed the right thing to invite them at Christmas.'

'Quite so,' said Henry. 'That all?'

'Oh, and little Miss Hooper.'

'Sent her measurements, did she?'

'You know what I mean,' said his sister, unperturbed. 'She always comes then. Besides, I expect she'll know the refugees. She does a lot of church work.'

'What sort of refugees are they?' asked Henry cautiously.

But that Wendy did not know.

Henry himself wasn't sure even after he'd first met them, and his brother-in-law was no help.

'Sorry, old man,' said that worthy as they foregathered in the drawing room, awaiting the arrival of the rest of the dinner guests on Christmas Eve. 'All I know is that this pair arrived from somewhere in Mitteleuropa last month with only what they stood up in.'

'Better out than in,' contributed Gordon Friar, the doctor, adding an old medical aphorism, 'like laudable pus.'

'I understand,' said Tom Witherington, 'that they only just got out, too. Skin of their teeth and all that.'

'As the poet so wisely said,' murmured Henry, '"The only certain freedom's in departure."'

'If you ask me,' said old Uncle George, a veteran of the Boer War, 'they did well to go while the going was good.'

'It's the sort of thing you can leave too late,' pronounced Dr Friar weightily. Leaving things too late was every doctor's nightmare.

'I don't envy 'em being where they are now,' said Tom. 'That camp they're in is pretty bleak, especially in the winter.'

This was immediately confirmed by Mrs Godiesky the moment she entered the room. She regarded the Witheringtons' glowing fire with deep appreciation. 'We 'ave been so cooald, so cooaald,' she said as she stared hungrily at the logs stacked by the open fireside. 'So very cooald …'

Her husband's English was slightly better, although also heavily accented. 'If we had not left when we did, then,' he opened his hands expressively, 'then who knows what would have become of us?'

'Who, indeed?' echoed Henry, who actually had a very much better idea than anyone else present of what might have become of the Godieskys had they not left their native heath when they did. Reports reaching the Foreign Office were very, very discouraging.

'They closed my university department down overnight,' explained Professor Hans Godiesky. 'Without any warning at all.'

'It was terrrrrible,' said Mrs Godiesky, holding her hands out to the fire as if she could never be warm again.

'What sort of a department was it, sir?' enquired Henry casually of the professor.

'Chemistry,' said the refugee, just as the two Watkins came in and the hanging mistletoe was put to good use. They were followed fairly quickly by Robert and Lorraine Steele from next door. The introductions in their case were more formal. Robert Steele was a good bit older than his wife, who was dressed in a very becoming mixture of red and dark green, though with a skirt that was rather shorter than either Wendy's or Dora's and even more noticeably so than that of Marjorie Friar, who was clearly no dresser.

'We're so glad you could get away in time,' exclaimed Wendy, while Tom busied himself with furnishing everyone with sherry. 'It must be difficult if there's late dispensing to be done.'

'No trouble these days,' boomed Robert Steele. 'I've got a young assistant now. He's a great help.'

Then Miss Hooper, whose skirt was longest of all, was shown in. She was out of breath and full of apology for being so late. 'Wendy, dear, I am so very sorry,' she fluttered. 'I'm afraid the Waits will be here in no time at all ...'

'And they won't wait,' said Henry guilelessly, 'will they?'

'If you ask me,' opined Tom Witherington, 'they won't get past the Royal Oak in a hurry.'

'The children are coming down in their dressing gowns to listen to the carols,' said Wendy, rightly ignoring both remarks. 'And I don't mind how tired they get tonight.'

'Who's playing Father Christmas?' asked Robert Steele jovially. He was a plump fellow, whose gaze rested fondly on his young wife most of the time.

'Not me,' said Tom Witherington.

'I am,' declared Henry. 'For my sins.'

'Then, when I am tackled on the matter,' said the children's father piously, 'I can put my hand on my heart and swear total innocence.'

'And how will you get out of giving an honest answer, Henry?' enquired Dora Watkins playfully.

'I shall hope,' replied Henry, 'to remain true to the traditions of the Foreign Service and give an answer that is at one and the same time absolutely correct and totally meaningless ...'

At which moment the sound of the dinner gong being struck came from the hall and presently the whole party moved through to the dining room, Uncle George giving the barometer a surreptitious tap on the way.

Henry Tyler studied the members of the party under cover of a certain amount of merry chat. It was part and parcel of his training that he could at one and the same time discuss Christmas festivities in England with poor Mrs Godiesky while covertly observing the other guests. Lorraine Steele was clearly the apple of her husband's eye, but he wasn't sure that the same could be said for Marjorie Friar, who emerged as a complainer and sounded – and looked – quite aggrieved with life.

Lorraine Steele though, was anything but dowdy. Henry decided her choice of red and green – Christmas colours – was a sign of a new outfit for yuletide.

He was also listening for useful clues about their homeland in the professor's conversation, while becoming aware that Tom's old Uncle George really was getting quite senile now and learning that the latest of Mrs Friar's succession of housemaids had given in her notice.

'And at Christmas, too,' she complained. 'So inconsiderate.'

Peter Watkins was displaying a modest pride in his Christmas present to his wife.

'Well,' he said in the measured tones of his profession of banking, 'personally, I'm sure that refrigerators are going to be the thing of the future.'

'There's nothing wrong with a good old-fashioned larder,' said Wendy stoutly, like the good wife she was. There was little chance of Tom Witherington being able to afford a refrigerator for a very long time. 'Besides, I don't think Cook would want to change her ways now. She's quite set in them, you know.'

'But think of the food we'll save,' said Dora. 'It'll never go bad now.'

'"Use it up, wear it out."' Something had stirred in old Uncle George's memory.

'"Make it do, do without or we'll send it to Belgium."'

'And you'll be more likely to avoid food poisoning, too,' said Robert Steele earnestly. 'Won't they, Dr Friar?'

'Yes, indeed,' the medical man agreed at once. 'There's always too much of that about and it can be very dangerous.'

The pharmacist looked at both the Watkins and said gallantly, 'I can't think of a better present.'

'But you did, darling,' chipped in Lorraine Steele brightly, 'didn't you?'

Henry was aware of an unspoken communication passing between the two Steeles; and then Lorraine Steele allowed her left hand casually to appear above the table. Her fourth finger was adorned with both a broad gold wedding ring and a ring on which was set a beautiful solitaire diamond.

'Robert's present,' she said rather complacently, patting her blonde Marcel waved hair and twisting the diamond ring round. 'Isn't it lovely?'

'I wanted her to wear it on her right hand,' put in Robert Steele, 'because she's left-handed, but she won't hear of it.'

'I should think not,' said Dora Watkins at once. 'The gold wedding ring sets it off so nicely.'

'That's what I say, too,' said Mrs Steele prettily, lowering her be-ringed hand out of sight again.

'Listen!' cried Wendy suddenly. 'It's the Waits. I can hear them now. Come along, everyone … it's mince pies and coffee all round in the hall afterwards.'

The Berebury carol-singers parked their lanterns outside the front door and crowded round the Christmas tree in the Witheringtons' entrance hall, their sheets of music held at the ready.

'Right,' called out their leader, a young man with a rather prominent Adam's apple. He began waving a little baton. 'All together now …'

The familiar words of 'Once in Royal David's City' soon rang out through the house, filling it with joyous sound. Henry caught a glimpse of a tear in Mrs Godiesky's eye; and noted a look of great nostalgia in little Miss Hooper's earnest expression. There must have been ghosts of Christmases Past in the scene for her, too.

Afterwards, when it became important to re-create the scene in his mind for the police, Henry could only place the Steeles at the back of the entrance hall with Dr Friar and Uncle George beside them. Peter and Dora Watkins had opted to stand a few steps up the stairs to the first-floor landing, slightly out of the press of people but giving them a good view. Mrs Friar was standing awkwardly in front of the leader of the choir. Of Professor Hans Godiesky there was no sign whatsoever while the carols were being sung.

Henry remembered noticing suppressed excitement in the faces of his niece and nephew perched at the top of the stairs and hoping it was the music that they had found entrancing and not the piles of mince pies awaiting them among the decorative smilax on the credenza at the back of the hall.

They – and everyone else – fell upon them nonetheless as soon as the last carol had been sung. There was a hot punch, too, carefully mulled to just the right temperature by Tom Witherington, for those old enough to partake of it, and homemade lemonade for the young.

Almost before the last choirboy had scoffed the last mince pie the party at the Witheringtons' broke up.

The pharmacist and his wife were the first to leave. They shook hands all round.

'I know it's early,' said Lorraine Steele apologetically, 'but I'm afraid Robert's poor old tummy's been playing him up again.' Henry, who had been expecting a rather limp paw, was surprised to find how firm her handshake was.

'If you'll forgive us,' said Lorraine's husband to Wendy, 'I think we'd better be on our way now.' Robert Steele essayed a glassy, strained smile, but to Henry's eye he looked more than a little white at the gills. Perhaps he, too, had spotted that the ring that was his Christmas present to his wife had got a nasty stain on the inner side of it.

The pair hurried off together in a flurry of farewells. Then the wispy Miss Hooper declared the evening a great success but said she wanted to check everything at St Faith's before the midnight service, and she, too, slipped away.

'What I want to know,' said Dora Watkins provocatively when the rest of the guests had reassembled in the drawing room and Edward and Jennifer had been sent back – very unwillingly – to bed, 'is whether it's better to be an old man's darling or a young man's slave?'

A frown crossed Wendy's face. 'I'm not sure,' she said seriously.

'I reckon our Mrs Steele's got her husband where she wants him, all right,' said Peter Watkins, 'don't you?'

'Come back, William Wilberforce, there's more work on slavery still to be done,' said Tom Witherington lightly. 'What about a nightcap, anyone?'

But there were no takers, and in a few moments the Friars, too, had left.

Wendy suddenly said she had decided against going to the Midnight Service after all and would see everyone in the morning. The rest of the household also opted for an early night and in the event Henry Tyler was the only one of the party to attend the Midnight Service at St Faith's church that night.

The words of the last carol, 'We Three Kings of Orient Are ...' were still ringing in his ears as he crossed the market square to the church. Henry wished that the Foreign Office had only kings to deal with: life would be simpler then. Dictators and presidents – particularly one president not so very many miles from 'perfidious Albion' – were much more unpredictable.

He hummed the words of the last verse of the carol as he climbed the church steps:

Myrrh is mine; its bitter perfume
Breathes a life of gathering gloom;
Sorrowing, sighing, bleeding, dying,
Sealed in the stone-cold tomb.

Perhaps, he thought, as he sought a back pew and his nostrils caught the inimical odour of a mixture of burning candles and church flowers, he should have been thinking of frankincense or even — when he saw the burnished candlesticks and altar cross — Melchior's gold ...

His private orisons were interrupted a few minutes later by a sudden flurry of activity near the front of the church, and he looked up in time to see little Miss Hooper being helped out by the two churchwardens.

'If I might just have a drink of water,' he heard her say before she was borne off to the vestry. 'I'll be all right in a minute. So sorry to make a fuss. So very sorry ...'

The rector's sermon was its usual interminable length and he was able to wish his congregation a happy Christmas as they left the church. As Henry walked back across the square he met Dr Friar coming out of the Steeles' house.

'Chap's collapsed,' he murmured. 'Severe epigastric pain and vomiting. Mrs Steele came round to ask me if I would go and see him. There was blood in the vomit and that frightened her.'

'It would,' said Henry.

'He's pretty ill,' said the doctor. 'I'm getting him into hospital as soon as possible.'

'Could it have been something he ate here?' said Henry, telling him about little Miss Hooper.

'Too soon to tell but quite possible,' said the doctor

gruffly. 'You'd better check how the others are when you get in. I rather think Wendy might be ill, too, from the look of her when we left, and I must say my wife wasn't feeling too grand when I went out. Ring me if you need me.'

Henry came back to a very disturbed house indeed, with several bedroom lights on. No one was very ill but Wendy and Mrs Godiesky were distinctly unwell. Dora Watkins was perfectly all right and was busy ministering to those that weren't.

Happily, there was no sound from the children's room and he crept in there to place a full stocking beside each of their beds. As he came back downstairs to the hall, he thought he heard an ambulance bell next door.

'The position will be clearer in the morning,' he said to himself, a Foreign Office man to the end of his fingertips.

It was.

Half the Witherington household had had a severe gastrointestinal upset during the night, and Robert Steele had died in the Berebury Royal Infirmary at about two o'clock in the morning.

When Henry met his sister on Christmas morning she had a very wan face indeed.

'Oh, Henry,' she cried, 'isn't it terrible about Robert Steele? And the rector says half the young Waits were ill in the night, too, and poor little Miss Hooper as well!'

'That lets the punch out, doesn't it?' said Henry thoughtfully, 'seeing as the youngsters weren't supposed to have any.'

'Cook says ...'

'Is she all right?' enquired Henry curiously.

'She hasn't been ill, if that's what you mean, but she's very upset.' Wendy sounded quite nervous. 'Cook says nothing like this has ever happened to her before.'

'It hasn't happened to her now,' pointed out Henry unkindly but Wendy wasn't listening.

'And Edward and Jennifer are all right, thank goodness,' said Wendy a little tearfully. 'Tom's beginning to feel better but I hear Mrs Friar's pretty ill still and poor Mrs Godiesky is feeling terrible. And as for Robert Steele ... I just don't know what to think. Oh, Henry, I feel it's all my fault.'

'Well, it wasn't the lemonade,' deduced Henry. 'Both children had lots. I saw them drinking it.'

'They had a mince pie each, too,' said their mother. 'I noticed. But some people who had them have been very ill since ...'

'Exactly, my dear. Some, but not all.'

'But what could it have been, then?' quavered Wendy. 'Cook is quite sure she only used the best of everything. And it stands to reason it was something that they ate here.' She struggled to put her fears into words. 'Here was the only place they all were.'

'It stands to reason that it was something they were given here,' agreed Henry, whom more than one ambassador had accused of pedantry, 'which is not quite the same thing.'

She stared at him. 'Henry, what do you mean?'

Inspector Milsom knew what he meant.

It was the evening of Boxing Day when he and Constable Bewman came to the Witheringtons' house.

'A number of people would appear to have suffered from

14

the effects of ingesting a small quantity of a dangerous substance at this address,' Milsom announced to the company assembled at his behest. 'One with fatal results.'

Mrs Godiesky shuddered. 'Me, I suffer a lot.'

'Me, too,' Peter Watkins chimed in.

'But not, I think, sir, your wife?' Inspector Milsom looked interrogatively at Dora Watkins.

'No, Inspector,' said Dora. 'I was quite all right.'

'Just as well,' said Tom Witherington. He still looked pale. 'We needed her to look after us.'

'Quite so,' said the inspector.

'It wasn't food poisoning, then?' said Wendy eagerly. 'Cook will be very pleased ...'

'It would be more accurate, madam,' said Inspector Milsom, who didn't have a cook to be in awe of, 'to say that there was poison in the food.'

Wendy paled. 'Oh ...'

'This dangerous substance of which you speak,' enquired Professor Godiesky with interest, 'is its nature known?'

'In England,' said the inspector, 'we call it corrosive sublimate ...'

'Mercury? Ah,' the refugee nodded sagely, 'that would explain everything.'

'Not quite everything, sir,' said the inspector mildly. 'Now, if we might see you one at a time, please.'

'This poison, Inspector,' said Henry after he had given his account of the carol-singing to the two policemen, 'I take it that it is not easily available?'

'That is correct, sir. But specific groups of people can obtain it.'

'Doctors and pharmacists?' hazarded Henry.

'And certain manufacturers ...'

'Certain ... Oh, Uncle George?' said Henry. 'Of course. There's plenty of mercury in thermometers.'

'The old gentleman is definitely a little confused, sir.'

'And Professors of Chemistry?' said Henry.

'In his position,' said the inspector judiciously, 'I should myself have considered having something with me just in case.'

'There being a fate worse than death,' agreed Henry swiftly, 'such as life in some places in Europe today. Inspector, might I ask what form this poison takes?'

'It's a white crystalline substance.'

'Easily confused with sugar?'

'It would seem easily enough,' said the policeman drily.

'And what you don't know, Inspector,' deduced Henry intelligently, 'is whether it was scattered on the mince pies ... I take it it was on the mince pies?'

'They were the most likely vehicle,' conceded the policeman.

'By accident or whether it was meant to make a number of people slightly ill or ...'

'Or,' put in Detective Constable Bewman keenly, 'one person very ill indeed?'

'Or,' persisted Henry quietly, 'both.'

'That is so.' He gave a dry cough. 'As it happens it did both make several people ill and one fatally so.'

'Which also might have been intended?' Nobody had ever called Henry slow.

'From all accounts,' said Milsom obliquely, 'Mr Steele had

a weak tummy before he ingested the corrosive sublimate of mercury.'

'Uncle George wasn't ill, was he?'

'No, sir, nor Dr Friar.' He gave his dry cough. 'I am told that Dr Friar never partakes of pastry.'

'Mrs Steele?'

'Slightly ill. She says she just had one mince pie. Mrs Watkins didn't have any. Nor did the professor.'

'"The one without the parsley," quoted Henry, '"is the one without the poison."'

'Just so, sir. It would appear at first sight from our immediate calculations quite possible that ...'

'Inspector, if you can hedge your bets as well as that before you say anything, we could find you a job in the Foreign Office.'

'Thank you, sir. As I was saying, sir, it is possible that the poison was only in the mince pies furthest from the staircase. Bewman here has done a chart of where the victims took their pies from.'

'Which would explain why some people were unaffected,' said Henry.

'Which might explain it, sir.' The inspector clearly rivalled Henry in his precision. 'The professor just wasn't there to take one at all. He says he went to his room to finish his wife's Christmas present. He was carving something for her out of a piece of old wood.'

'"Needs must when the devil drives,"' responded Henry absently. He was still thinking. 'It's a pretty little problem, as they say.'

'Means and opportunity would seem to be present,' murmured Milsom.

'That leaves motive, doesn't it?' said Henry.

'The old gentleman mightn't have had one, seeing he's as he is, sir, if you take my meaning and of course we don't know anything about the professor and his wife, do we, sir? Not yet.'

'Not a thing.'

'That leaves the doctor ...'

'I'd've murdered Mrs Friar years ago,' announced Henry cheerfully, 'if she had been my wife.'

'And Mrs Steele.' There was a little pause and then Inspector Milsom said, 'I understand the new young assistant at the pharmacy is more what you might call a contemporary of Mrs Steele.'

'Ah, so that's the way the wind's blowing, is it?'

'And then, sir,' said the policeman, 'after motive there's still what we always call down at the station the fourth dimension of crime ...'

'And what might that be, Inspector?'

'Proof.' He got up to go. 'Thank you for your help, sir.'

Henry sat quite still after the two policemen had gone, his memory teasing him. Someone he knew had been poisoned with corrosive sublimate of mercury, served to him in tarts. By a tart, too, if history was to be believed.

No, not someone he knew.

Someone he knew of.

Someone they knew about at the Foreign Office because it had been a political murder, a famous political murder set round an eternal triangle ...

Henry Tyler sought out Professor Godiesky and explained.

'It was recorded by contemporary authors,' Henry said, 'that when the tarts poisoned with mercury were delivered to the Tower of London for Sir Thomas Overbury, the fingernail of the woman delivering them had accidentally been poked through the pastry ...'

The professor nodded sapiently. 'And it was stained black?'

'That's right,' said Henry. History did have some lessons to teach, in spite of what Henry Ford had said. 'But it would wash off?'

'Yes,' said Hans Godiesky simply.

'So I'm afraid that doesn't get us anywhere, does it?'

The academic leaned forward slightly, as if addressing a tutorial. 'There is, however, one substance on which mercury always leaves its mark.'

'There is?' said Henry.

'Its — how do you say it in English? — its ineradicable mark.'

'That's how we say it,' said Henry slowly. 'And which substance, sir, would that be?'

'Gold, Mr Tyler. Mercury stains gold.'

'For ever?'

'For ever.' He waved a hand. 'An amalgam is created.'

'And I,' Henry gave a faint smile, 'I was foolish enough to think it was diamonds that were for ever.'

'Pardon?'

'Nothing, Professor. Nothing at all. Forgive me, but I think I may be able to catch the inspector and tell him to look to the lady. And her gold wedding ring.'

'Look to the lady?' The refugee was now totally bewildered. 'I do not understand ...'

'It's a quotation.'

'Ach, sir, I fear I am only a scientist.'

'There's a better quotation,' said Henry, 'about looking to science for the righting of wrongs. I rather think Mrs Steele may have looked to science, too, to – er – improve her lot. And if she carefully scattered the corrosive sublimate over some mince pies and not others it would have been with her left hand ...'

'Because she was left-handed,' said the professor immediately. 'That I remember. And you think one mince pie would have had – I know the English think this important – more than its fair share?'

'I do. Then all she had to do was to give her husband that one and Bob's your uncle. Clever of her to do it in someone else's house.'

Hans Godiesky looked totally mystified. 'And who was Bob?'

'Don't worry about Bob,' said Henry from the door. 'Think about Melchior and his gold instead.'

Hot Money

Carter Dickson

Just before closing time on a Tuesday afternoon in December, a saloon car drew up before the St James's office of the City and Provincial Bank, and four men got out. Lights were burning inside the bank, but the day was raw and murky. Two of the newcomers went to the counter, where they accosted the cashiers with pistol-muzzles cradled over their arms. The third, who wore no hat or coat, walked behind the counter; and, before anybody knew what he was doing, began quietly drawing the blinds on the windows.

The fourth, who had taken a 45-calibre revolver out of his overcoat pocket, spoke with great clearness.

'You know why we're here,' he said. 'Just keep quiet and nothing will happen to you.'

One of the clerks, a youngster, laughed; and was instantly shot through the chest with a silenced gun.

The noise it made was no louder than that of slapping two

cupped palms together, a kind of *thock*. The clerk tumbled sideways, rattling against a scales, and they heard his body strike the floor. Then all noise seemed to die away under the bright, hard lights, except the sound of the newcomers' footsteps on the marble floor.

'That's right,' said the man who had first spoken. 'Just keep quiet and nothing will happen to you.'

The thing was incredible; but it was happening. Possibly every man in the bank, now staring in various twisted positions with hands in the air, had seen it happen in a film, and had smiled at it as being confined to another continent. But with great precision the man who had drawn the blinds was now clearing out the safe, transferring what he wanted to a neat leather bag. Outside bustled the traffic of St James's; passers-by saw a closed bank, and thought nothing of it. By the third minute it had become unbearable. The manager, risking it, ducked under the counter for a gun, and was shot down. Then the leader of the gang leaned close to a young clerk named John Parrish, and said:

'Thanks, kid. You'll get your cut.'

Like four well-trained ghosts, the raiders came together and melted out into the street. Their car was away from the kerb before the alarm sounded.

Now the robbery of the City and Provincial Bank failed because of one small but important fact. In England you can rob quite easily; you can even, if you do not mind risking the gallows, rob with violence; but you cannot make a getaway afterwards. 'Skipper' Morgan, late of Cicero, Illinois, might be excused for not realising this. But Pudge Henderson,

Slugger Dean and Bill Stein, all of whom knew Dartmoor as the rest of us know our own homes, should have realised it. Possibly they expected the very daring of the raid to bring it off for them, and they changed cars three times before, early that evening, two Flying Squad cars cut them off on the road to Southampton.

Skipper Morgan wanted to shoot it out, and was brought down in a flying tackle which broke his arm. But here the police met a snag: of £23,000 in cash and bonds, not one penny was found on the fugitives.

Chief Inspector Ames visited Skipper Morgan that night.

'You're in bad, Skipper,' he said pleasantly. 'One of those fellows you shot is likely to die. Even if he pulls through, you can reckon on a good long stretch.'

The other said nothing, though he looked murderous. It was Ames who had broken his arm.

'I don't say it'd help you,' pursued the chief inspector, 'if you told us what you did with that money. But it might, Skipper. It *might*. And you might tell us whether that young clerk at the bank, the one you said would get his cut, was in it with you.'

'Dirty little rat,' said the Skipper, out of pure spite and malice. 'Sure he was in it. But I want to see my lawyer; that's what I want.'

So they detained John Parrish. To Marjorie Dawson he wrote: 'Don't you believe a word of it. Cheer up.'

A solicitor for Morgan was speedily produced. This was none other than Mr Ireton Bowlder, that aloof gentleman with the aristocratic nose and the wide clientèle. Scotland Yard regarded him with disfavour, because he never failed to put their backs up. True, there was little that even Mr Ireton Bowlder could do for the prisoners; but he contrived to suggest, with a fishy smile and a sad shake of the head, that they would leave the court without a stain on their characters. Still the stolen money was not forthcoming.

'It's one of two things, sir,' Chief Inspector Ames told the assistant commissioner. 'They've hidden it, or they've turned it over to a fence.'

'A fence for stolen money?'

'And bonds,' said Ames. 'Nothing easier. Of course we've got the numbers of the notes, fivers and above. But they can easily be disposed of abroad: people are buying and hoarding English money, and they don't necessarily enquire where it comes from. I know of two fences like that, and I hear there's a third operating who's the biggest in the business. Getting rid of "hot" money used to be difficult; but it's simple now. It's more than a new kind of racket; it's a new kind of big business. The state of Europe being what it is, thousands of people are trying to get out of there and into England without their authorities knowing they've got any money at all. Hoarding English money is the best way to do it. If we could get a line on who's doing this—'

'Any suspicions?'

'Yes, sir,' answered Ames promptly. 'Ireton Bowlder.'

The assistant commissioner whistled. 'If it only could be!' he said, with dreamy relish. 'Lord, if it only could be! But be careful, Ames; he's got a lot of influence. And what makes you think it's Bowlder, anyway?'

'It's all underground so far,' Ames admitted. 'But that's what the boys say. Now, we nabbed Morgan and his mob just outside a village called Crawleigh. Bowlder's got a country house only a mile from there. Bowlder was at his country house on Tuesday night, though as a rule he only goes down at weekends. Skipper Morgan was down there twice in the week before the robbery. It doesn't prove anything. But taken with the rest of the rumours—'

'What about the boy Parrish?'

Ames grinned. 'Had nothing to do with it, sir. It was Morgan's temper, that's all, or Morgan's idea of a joke. I'm convinced of it, and so is the bank. But Parrish might be useful.'

Just how useful Chief Inspector Ames did not realise until the following day, when Miss Marjorie Dawson came hurrying up to town.

She was a quiet, fair-haired girl, pretty yet unobtrusive, though now strung up to fighting pitch. Her hazel eyes had a directness of gaze which was as good as a handclasp; she had, even in this difficulty, a sense of humour. She told the chief inspector things which made him swear.

But, after a half-hour interview, it was not to the assistant commissioner that Ames took her. He took her to a door on the ground floor labelled *D3: Colonel March.*

'Colonel March,' he said, 'let me introduce Miss Marjorie Dawson. Miss Dawson is engaged to be married to young Parrish. She's now employed as secretary to Ireton Bowlder's aunt—'

'Not any longer,' said the girl, smiling faintly. 'Sacked yesterday.'

'And she says Bowlder's got the City and Provincial Bank money.'

Colonel March was a large, amiable man, with a speckled face, a bland eye, and a large-bowled pipe projecting from under a cropped moustache. He rocked on his heels before the fire, and seemed puzzled.

'I am delighted to hear it,' he said formally. 'But why come to me? This, Miss Dawson, is the Queer Complaints Department. Business has been bad lately; and I should be very glad to tackle the problem of a blue pig or a ghost in the garden. But, if you've landed Ireton, why come to me?'

'Because it's a queer complaint, right enough,' said Ames grimly. 'What Miss Dawson tells us is impossible.'

'Impossible?'

Marjorie Dawson looked from one to the other of them, and drew a deep breath of relief. Colour had come back into her face.

'I hope you're being frank with me,' she said. She appealed to Colonel March. 'Inspector Ames tells me that you haven't really got a case against John Parrish, and don't mean to hold him—'

'No, no; you can have him whenever you want him,' said Ames with impatience.

'—but I came up here after somebody's blood,' the girl admitted. 'You see, the local police wouldn't believe me; and yet it's true, every word of it.'

'The money vanished in front of their eyes,' said Ames.

'One moment,' said Colonel March, with an air of refreshed interest. He pushed out chairs for them. 'Disappearing money. That is better; that is distinctly better. Tell me about it.'

'It was at Greenacres,' said the girl, so eager to tell the

story that they had to guide her to the chair. 'Greenacres is Mr Bowlder's country house. As Mr Ames told you, I'm Miss Bowlder's secretary; she keeps house for her nephew.

'I'm not going to tell you what I felt when I heard about the robbery. The first I knew of it was when I opened the newspaper at the breakfast table on Wednesday, and saw John's name staring up at me — as though he'd committed a murder or something. I couldn't believe it. I knew it was a mistake of some kind. But I thought Mr Bowlder might know—'

'Might know?' prompted Colonel March.

She hesitated, her forehead puckered. 'Well, not that, exactly. I thought he might be able to help me, being a solicitor. Or at least that he would know what to do.

'It was barely half past eight in the morning. I was the only one up in the house, except servants; Miss Bowlder doesn't get down until nine. Then I remembered that Mr Bowlder had come down to Greenacres the afternoon before, and I could go to him straight away.

'That's how it happened. You see, when Mr Bowlder is at Greenacres he always has nine o'clock breakfast with his aunt: very dutiful and all that. Any letters that come for him in the morning are always put in his study — which is at the back of the house. Before he goes in to breakfast, he always goes to the study to see if there are any letters. So back I went to the study, to catch him alone before he went to breakfast. I didn't knock; I just opened the door and walked in. And I got a shock that I thought I must be seeing things.

'The study is a large, rather bare room, with two windows looking out over a terrace. It has recently been painted, by the way, which is rather important. It was a bright, cold, quiet morning; and the sun was pouring in. There was a bust of somebody or other on the mantelpiece, and a big flat-topped desk in the centre of the room. Of course, I hadn't expected to find anybody there. But Mr Bowlder was sitting at the table, fully dressed. And spread out in rows on the table were at least twenty packets of banknotes of all denominations. Nearly every packet was fastened with a little paper band with *City and Provincial Bank* printed on it.

'I simply stood and stared. My head was full of the City and Provincial Bank. And, anyway, it's not his own bank.

'Then Mr Bowlder turned round and saw me. The sun was behind his head and I didn't get a good view of his face; but all of a sudden his fingers crisped up as though he were going to scratch with them. Then he got up and ran at me. I jumped outside; he slammed the door, and bolted it on the inside.'

She paused.

'Go on, Miss Dawson,' said Colonel March in a curious voice.

'It takes a long time to tell,' she went on rather blankly, 'but in a second or two I put together a whole lot of things. Skipper Morgan's gang had been arrested just outside our village; the paper said so. Morgan's picture was in the paper, and I knew I had seen him at Greenacres the week before. John had been down there to visit me, too. I suppose Morgan saw him there, and that's why Morgan made such very funny jokes about John when the bank was robbed. It was all a kind of whirl in my head; but it came together as a dead certainty.

'There is a telephone in the hall just outside Mr Bowlder's study. I sat down and rang up the local police.'

Here she looked at them with some defiance.

'What I was afraid of was that Mr Bowlder would come out of the room and take the money away and hide it somewhere before the police arrived. I didn't see how I could stop him if he did. But he didn't even come out of the study. That worried me horribly, because the room was as quiet as a grave and I wondered what he might be up to. I like people to *do* something.

'Then I thought: "Suppose he got out of a window?" But I remembered something about that. As I told you, the woodwork of that room had been painted only a few days before. It wasn't the best of painting jobs; and as a result both windows were so stuck that it was impossible to open them. Annie had been complaining about it the day before; they were to have been seen to that very day. So, when the police arrived — I could hardly believe my good luck — Mr Bowlder was still in that room with the money.

'It was an inspector and a sergeant of the local police. They were on hot bricks, because Mr Bowlder is an important man; but the Morgan gang had been caught near there and they weren't taking any chances. While I was trying to explain, Mr Bowlder opened the door of the study. He was as pleasant and sad-faced as ever.

'He said: "Money? What money?"

'I explained all over again, and I'm afraid I got a bit incoherent about it. But I told them the money was still in the study, because Mr Bowlder hadn't left it.

'He said — and don't I remember it! — "Gentlemen, this

young lady is suffering from optical illusions. At nine o'clock in the morning this is a pity. I am aware that you have no search warrant, Inspector, but you are at liberty to make as thorough a search of this room as you like. How much money was there, Miss Dawson?"

'I said thousands and thousands of pounds: it sounded wrong even as I said it. Mr Bowlder laughed.

'He said: "Thousands and thousands of pounds, eh? Gentlemen, if you can find any money in this room – apart from a few shillings on my person – I will donate it all to police charities. But there is no money here."

'And there wasn't. Enough money to fill a suitcase; and yet it wasn't there.'

Colonel March frowned. 'You mean the police didn't find it?'

'I mean it wasn't there to be found. It had just vanished.'

'That's as true as gospel,' declared Chief Inspector Ames with vehemence. 'I rang them up half an hour ago and talked to Inspector Daniels. Search? They had the whole place to pieces! Bowlder sat and smoked cigarettes and egged them on. They even got an architect in to make certain there were no secret cavities anywhere in the room.'

'And?'

'There weren't any. There wasn't a hiding place for so much as a pound note, let alone a sackful of the stuff. The point is, what's to be done? I don't think Miss Dawson is lying; but all that money couldn't vanish into thin air. How could it?'

Colonel March was pleased. He relighted his pipe; he rocked on his heels before the fire; then, becoming conscious of the impropriety, he coughed and tried to conceal the fact that he was pleased.

'I beg your pardon,' he said. 'But this is the best thing I have encountered since the Chevalier C. Auguste Dupin (you recall?) went after the purloined letter. Ahem. Now let us see. We establish that there are no secret panels, cavities, or other flummery. Windows?'

'Just as Miss Dawson said. The windows were so stuck that two men couldn't move 'em. Nothing could have been taken out of the room like that.'

'Fireplace?'

'Bricked up. They don't use it, because the room is centrally heated. Bricks solidly cemented and untouched. No possible hiding place in or round the fireplace.'

'Furniture?'

Ames consulted his notebook. 'One flat-topped table, one small table, two easy chairs, one straight chair, one bookcase, one lamp standard, one standing ashtray. You can take it for granted that not one of those got away without the closest examination; and nothing was hidden in any of them. Anything to add to that, Miss Dawson?'

Marjorie shook her head.

'No. And it wasn't in the carpet or the curtains, or behind the pictures, or in the leaves of the books, or even in the bust I mentioned; not that you could put all that money there, anyway. It just wasn't there.' She clenched her hands. 'But you do believe me, don't you?'

'Miss Dawson,' said Ames slowly, 'I don't know. You're certain Bowlder didn't leave the study at any time before the police arrived?'

'Positive.'

'He couldn't have slipped out?'

'No. I was in front of the door all the time. It's true, Inspector. What reason would I have for lying to you? It's only got me the sack, and it hasn't helped John. I've thought and thought about it. I thought of the trick, too, of hiding a thing by leaving it in plain sight, where nobody notices it. But you certainly couldn't leave the City and Provincial Bank money in plain sight without anybody noticing it.'

'Well, it beats me,' admitted the chief inspector. 'But then that's why we're here. It's impossible! Daniels swears there wasn't an inch of that room they didn't go over with a fine-tooth comb. And yet I believe you, because I've got a feeling Bowlder has been too smart for us somehow. Any ideas, Colonel?'

Colonel March sniffed at his pipe.

'I was just wondering,' he muttered; and then a doubtful grin broke over his face. 'I am still wondering. Look here, Miss Dawson; you are sure there was *no* article of furniture in that room you haven't described to us?'

'If you mean things like ashtrays or desk ornaments—'

'No, no; I mean quite a large article of furniture.'

'I'm certain there wasn't. There couldn't very well be a large article of furniture that nobody would see.'

'I wonder,' said Colonel March. 'Is Mr Bowlder still at Greenacres? Excellent! I very much want to speak to him; and I want to see his study.'

Under a sky heavy with threatening snow, the police car left Scotland Yard early in the afternoon. It contained Chief Inspector Ames and the plain-clothes man who was driving in the front seat, with Marjorie Dawson and Colonel March in the rear seat. To the girl's protests that she wished to remain in London with Parrish, Colonel March was deaf; he said there was time enough. At four o'clock they drove into the grounds of an ugly but highly substantial and highly respectable country house in Victorian Gothic.

Colonel March stood up as the car stopped in the drive.

'Where,' he asked, 'are the windows of the study?'

'At the back,' said Marjorie. 'You take the path round to the left—'

'Let's take it,' said Colonel March.

Dusk was coming on, but no lights showed at Greenacres. They circled the house under the blast of an east wind, Colonel March stumping ahead with his coat collar turned up and an old tweed cap pulled low on his forehead. Climbing stone-flagged steps to a terrace, they looked into the nearer of the study windows; and came face to face with Mr Ireton Bowlder looking out at them.

One of Bowlder's hands flattened out against the glass with white fingers. The other hand, which was wrapped in a handkerchief, he thrust into his pocket. In the twilight he looked nervous and a trifle greenish of countenance.

'Good afternoon,' said Colonel March politely. The wind whipped the words away; and Bowlder inside the glass was as silent as a fish in an aquarium, though his lips moved. Then Bowlder raised the window.

'I said good afternoon,' repeated Colonel March. Before Bowlder could move back he had reached out and shaken hands with him through the window. 'You know most of us, I think.'

'Yes,' said Bowlder, looking at Marjorie. 'What do you want?'

Colonel March leaned against the ledge of the window.

'I thought you would like to know,' he said, 'that the manager of the City and Provincial Bank was a little better this morning. That will probably make the charge against five persons something a little less than murder.'

'Indeed. The fifth is young Parrish, I suppose?'

'No,' said Colonel March. 'The fifth is probably yourself.'

Again wind whipped round the corner of the house, ruffling Bowlder's neat hair. But Bowlder himself was not ruffled. He regarded them with a pale and sceptical smile; then he began to close the window.

'Better not,' the colonel advised. 'We're coming in.'

'You have a warrant?'

'Oh, yes. That window is now in working order, I see. Robinson,' he looked at the plain-clothes man, 'will climb through and stay with you while we go round by the front door.'

By the time they reached the study, Bowlder had turned on a standard lamp by the table, upon which it threw a bright light, though most of the room was left in shadow. The room was exactly as Marjorie Dawson had described.

'Now, then,' said Bowlder quietly, 'will you explain what you mean by this nonsense about a charge?'

'If,' said Colonel March, 'the City and Provincial money is found here, you're likely to be charged with Skipper Morgan. That is what I meant.'

'Gentlemen – and Miss Dawson – listen to me. How many times have I got to submit to this? You don't really mean you want to make still another search?'

'Yes.'

'Look round you,' said Bowlder. 'Take a long, careful look. Can you think of any place that could have been overlooked the first time?'

Chief Inspector Ames had to admit to himself that he couldn't. But Colonel March, instead of searching for a secret in the room, lowered himself into an easy chair by the table. Removing his cap and turning down the collar of his coat, he faced them with a kind of sleepy affability.

'In order to show you what I mean,' he went on, 'I must point out one of the curiously blind spots in the human mind. Has it ever occurred to you, Ames, that there's one piece of furniture in a room that nobody ever notices?'

'No, sir, it hasn't,' said Ames. 'You mean it's hidden?'

'On the contrary, I mean that it may be right there in front of everyone's eyes. But few people will ever see it.'

'Are you trying to tell me,' asked the chief inspector, 'that there's such a thing as an invisible piece of furniture?'

'A mentally invisible piece of furniture,' returned Colonel March. 'Would you like proof of it? You have one, my boy, in the sitting room of your own flat. I imagine there's one in the bedroom as well. It is under your eyes all the time. But suppose I said to you: "Give me a list of every piece of furniture in your flat." You would then give a list of things down to the smallest lampshade or ashtray; but I am willing to bet you would omit this whacking great object—'

Chief Inspector Ames looked round rather wildly. But his eye fell on Mr Ireton Bowlder, and he checked himself. Bowlder, who had been lighting a cigarette, dropped the match on the floor. Under the bright light of the lamp his forehead shone with sweat; and he was not smiling.

Ames stared at him.

'Whether or not I understand you,' he said, 'by Jupiter, that fellow does!'

'Yes. I thought he would,' agreed Colonel March, and got to his feet. 'That's where he has hidden the money, you see.'

'Oh, what on earth are you talking about?' cried Marjorie Dawson. She could keep herself in hand no longer, and she almost screamed. 'What could be invisible? What is there we can't see? What part of the room is it in? What's the size of it? What's the colour of it, even?'

'As for size,' replied the Colonel, 'it may vary a good deal, but in this case it is about three feet high, two and a half feet long, and three or four inches deep. In colour it is sometimes painted a bright gilt; but in this case the object is painted a modest brown.'

'*What?*'

'I mean,' said Colonel March, 'a steam radiator. Particularly a dummy radiator like that one in the corner over there.'

Ireton Bowlder made a run for the door, but he was tripped and brought down by PC Robinson. They were compelled to use handcuffs when they took him away.

'The possibilities of a dummy radiator, used for concealing something inside,' said Colonel March, when they were on their way home, 'deserve the attention of our best crooks. It is very nearly a perfect hiding place. It is compact. It will hold a great deal of swag. And it is the one thing we never seem to notice, even if we happen to be looking at it.

'Nobody, you see, regards it as a piece of furniture at all; certainly not as a piece of furniture in which anything could possibly be concealed. Inspector Daniels never looked twice at the radiator in Bowlder's study, and it is difficult to blame him. The radiator gave out heat, like an honest radiator; it was of iron; it seemed solid; it was clamped to the floor.

'You can buy one of them easily enough. They are really disguised oil stoves; portable, with several concealed burners, one under each coil. I have never forgotten the shock I received, sitting comfortably by a steaming radiator in the house of a friend of mine, when it suddenly occurred to me that the house was not centrally heated. Bowlder's radiator, as you saw, was a more elaborate affair, but one that could be constructed without difficulty. Two of the coils contained no burners, were invisibly hinged at the back, and formed a hollow receptacle as large as he could wish. The house was centrally heated, so that a mere radiator aroused no suspicion whatever. It was, in short, a private safe without lock or combination, but so commonplace as to defy suspicion. I have been waiting for somebody to try the trick; and lo, somebody did.'

Marjorie Dawson looked at him enquiringly.

'You mean you expected to find one of those things when we went down to Greenacres?' she asked.

'I am the Department of Queer Complaints,' said Colonel March with apology, 'and I was on the lookout for it as soon as central heating was reported in that room. I wasn't sure, of course, until we talked to Bowlder through the study window. The banknotes would get rather warm, you can understand, from being in a compartment next to the oil burner. They wouldn't scorch, any more than our clothes scorch when we put them to dry on top of an ordinary radiator, but they would be tolerably warm; and so would the fastenings when Bowlder opened his safe. That was why he had to wrap a handkerchief round his right hand. And it was Chief Inspector Ames, with unerring intuition, who hit on the real clue long before it ever came to me.'

'I did?' demanded Ames.

'Yes,' said Colonel March. 'You told me, with an accuracy beyond your wildest knowledge, that the money was hot.'

It Takes Two ...

Cyril Hare

It takes two to make a murder. The psychology of the murderer has been analysed often enough; what qualifies a man to be murdered is a subject less frequently discussed, though sometimes, perhaps, more interesting.

Derek Walton, who was killed by Ted Brackley on a dark December evening in Boulter's Mews, Mayfair, was uniquely fitted for his part in that rather sordid little drama. He was a well-built young man, five feet eight inches high, with dark hair and hazel eyes. He had a toothbrush moustache and walked with a slight limp. He was employed by Mallard's, that small and thriving jewellers' establishment just off Bond Street, and at the time of his death had in his pocket a valuable parcel of diamonds which Mallard had told him to take to Birmingham to be reset. The diamonds, naturally enough, provided the motive for the murder, but Walton would not have died exactly when and how he did had he been fat, or blue-eyed, or more than five feet nine, for Brackley was a cautious man. There was one other fact in Walton's life which finally loaded the scales against him – he was given to gambling on the dogs, and fairly heavily in debt.

There was very little about Walton that Brackley did not know, after a period of intense study which had extended now for a matter of months. Patiently and remorselessly he had studied his quarry in every aspect. Every detail in his physical appearance, down to the least trick of gesture, gait or accent, had been noted with a more than lover-like devotion. A creature of habit, Walton was an easy subject for observation, and his goings-out and comings-in had long since been learned by heart. Brackley knew all about the lodgings in West London where he lived, the pubs he frequented, the bookies he patronised, his furtive and uninteresting love affairs. More than once he had followed him to Birmingham, where his parents lived, and to the very doors of Watkinshaws, the manufacturing jewellers there who carried out the exquisite designs on which old Nicholas Mallard's reputation had been built. In fact, Brackley reflected, as he waited in the shadows of Boulter's Mews, about the only thing he did not precisely know about Walton was what went on inside his head. But that was an irrelevant detail, as irrelevant as are the emotions of a grazing stag to the stalker the moment before he presses the trigger.

Walton was later than usual that evening. Brackley took a quick glance at his wristwatch and frowned. In ten minutes' time the constable on his beat was due at the end of the mews. He decided that he could allow himself another two minutes at the most. After that, the margin of safety would be too small, and the operation would have to be called off for the night. A later opportunity would offer itself no doubt, and he could afford to wait, but it would be a pity, for the conditions were otherwise ideal. The shops had closed and the sound of the last assistants and office workers hurrying home had long since died away. The tide of pleasure traffic to the West End had not yet set in. A faint mist, too thin to be called a fog, had begun to rise from the damp pavements. What on earth was keeping Walton back?

The two minutes had still thirty seconds to run when Brackley heard what he was waiting for. Fifty yards away, in Fentiman Street, he heard the back door of Mallard's close, and the rattle of the key in the lock as Walton secured the premises behind him. Evidently he was the last out of the shop as usual. There was a pause, long enough to make Brackley wonder whether his quarry had defeated him by deciding to walk out into Bond Street instead of taking his usual shortcut through the mews; and then he heard the unmistakable limping footsteps coming towards him. He realised, as he slid back into the open doorway behind him, that the steps were decidedly faster than usual. That was unfortunate, since everything depended on precise timing. Now, at the critical moment, so long prepared, so carefully rehearsed, there would have to be an element of improvisation, and improvisation meant risk. Brackley had been to endless pains to eliminate risk in this affair. He resented having any put upon him.

After all, he need not have worried. The business went perfectly according to plan. As Walton passed the doorway

Brackley stepped out behind him. A quick glance to either side assured him that the mews was deserted. He took two soundless paces in time with his victim. Then the rubber-handled cosh struck once, behind the right ear, precisely as he had intended, and Walton pitched forward without a groan.

The body never touched the ground. Even as he delivered the blow, Brackley had followed up and caught it round the waist with his left hand. For an instant he stood supporting it, and then with a quick heave lifted it onto his shoulder and carried it into the entry from which he had emerged. The whole incident had not taken more than ten seconds. There had been no sound, except the dull impact of the blow itself and the faint clatter made by the suitcase which Walton had been carrying as it fell to the ground. The case itself and Walton's hat, lying side by side in the gutter, were the only evidence of what had occurred. Within as short a space of time again Brackley had darted out once more and retrieved them. The door closed silently behind him. Boulter's Mews was as silent as a grave and as empty as a cenotaph.

Panting slightly from his exertions, but completely cool, Brackley went swiftly to work by the light of an electric torch. He was standing in a small garage of which he was the legitimate tenant, and he had laid the body upon a rug behind the tailboard of a small van of which he was the registered owner. The cosh was beside it. There had been little bleeding, and he had made sure that what there was had been absorbed by the rug. Quickly and methodically he went through Walton's pockets. The diamonds, as he expected, were in a small, sealed packet in an inside coat pocket. A brown leather wallet contained some of Walton's business cards, a few pound notes and some personal papers. Then came an agreeable surprise. In a hip pocket, along with a cheap cigarette case, was a thick bundle of pound notes. Brackley did not stop to count them, but he judged that there were a hundred of them, more or less. He grinned in the darkness. Other arrangements had compelled him to allow Walton to go to the dog races unattended during the last two weeks. Evidently his luck there had turned at last – and just in time. He stuffed the notes along with the rest into his own pockets and then minutely examined the appearance of the dead man from head to foot.

What he saw satisfied him completely. Walton, that creature of habit, had dressed for his work that day in exactly the same clothes as usual. The clothes that Brackley was now wearing were identically the same. Brackley's shoulders were not quite so broad as Walton's, but a little padding in the shoulders of the overcoat had eliminated that distinction. Brackley stood only five feet seven inches in his socks, but in the shoes he had prepared for the occasion he looked as tall as Walton had been. A touch of dye had corrected the slight difference between the colours of their hair. Brackley stroked the toothbrush moustache which he had been cultivating for the last month and decided that the resemblance would pass.

No casual observer would have doubted that the man who limped out of the southern end of the mews carrying a small suitcase was other than the man who had entered its northern end a scant five minutes earlier. Certainly the newspaper seller in Bond Street did not. Automatically he extended Walton's usual paper, automatically he made the same trite observation he had made to Walton every evening, and heard without comment the reply which came to him in a very fair imitation of Walton's Midlands accent. By a piece of good fortune, a policeman was passing at the time. He would remember the incident if the newspaperman did not. Walton's presence in Bond Street was now firmly established; it remained to lay a clear trail to Birmingham.

A taxi appeared at just the right moment. Brackley stopped it and in a voice pitched loud enough to reach the constable's ear told the man to drive to Euston. For good measure, he asked him if he thought he could catch the 6.55 train to Birmingham, and expressed exaggerated relief when the driver assured him that he had time to spare.

Walton always took the 6.55 to Birmingham, and travelled first class at his firm's expense. Brackley did the same. By a little touch of fussiness and a slightly exaggerated tip, he contrived to leave an impression on the porter who carried his bag to the train which he hoped would be remembered. Walton always dined in the restaurant car. Brackley was in two minds whether to carry his impersonation as far as that. The car was well lighted, and some of these waiters had long memories and sharp eyes. He decided to venture, and had no cause to regret it. The attendant asked him if he would have a Guinness as usual, and remarked that it was some time since he had seen him on that train and hadn't he grown a little thinner? Brackley, taking care not to show his teeth, which were more irregular than Walton's, agreed that he had, and drank off his Guinness in the rather noisy manner that Walton always affected. He left the dining car just before the train ran into New Street, taking care not to overdo the limp.

As he made his way back to his compartment he reflected with the conscious pride of the artist that the campaign had been a complete success. What was left to be done was comparatively simple, and that had been prepared with the same methodical detail as the rest. At New Street station Walton would abruptly and finally disappear. His suitcase would go into the railway cloakroom, to be discovered, no doubt, in due course when the hue and cry for him had begun. Walking through carefully reconnoitred back streets, Brackley would make his way from the station to the furnished room where a change of clothes and identity awaited him. Next day, in London, the van in which Walton's body was now stiffening would drive quietly from Boulter's Mews to the garage in Kent, where a resting place was prepared for its burden beneath six inches of newly laid concrete. There would be nothing to connect that unobtrusive journey with a young man last seen a hundred miles the other side of London.

The trail would end at Birmingham, and there enquiries would begin – and end. Walton's parents, who were expecting him for the night, were unlikely to inform the police when he failed to arrive. The first alarm would probably be sounded by Watkinshaws, when the diamonds they were expecting were not delivered in the morning. Whether Walton's disappearance was held to be voluntary or not was an academic question which it would be interesting to follow in the newspaper reports. But he judged that when the state of Walton's finances was revealed the police would be cynical enough to write him off as yet another trusted employee who had yielded to temptation when his debts got out of hand. A hunt for a live Walton, fugitive from justice, would be an additional assurance that Walton dead would rest undisturbed.

As the lights of New Street showed through the carriage windows, Brackley tested in his mind the links of the chain he had forged. Were they adequate? The newspaper seller — the taxi driver — the porter — the waiter — would they come forward when required? Would they remember him with certainty? Human testimony was fallible, after all, and the chain might snap somewhere. Yet short of proclaiming himself aloud as Walton on the station platform there was nothing further he could do.

He was gazing absently at the elderly lady who shared his compartment when it suddenly came to his mind that there was still something that might be done, a last artistic touch to put the issue beyond a doubt. Her suitcase was on the rack above her head, and his — Walton's — lay next to it. He noticed for the first time that they were remarkably alike. (It was a cheap line from Oxford Street, he knew. He had bought the twin of it himself, in case it was wanted for his impersonation but he had not needed it.) Seizing the chance which a kind fate provided, he rose quickly when the train stopped, took her bag from its place and stepped out onto the platform.

It worked like a charm. Before he had limped half the length of the train his late companion had overtaken him, carrying his case and calling on him to stop.

'Excuse me,' she piped, in a high, carrying voice, 'but you've made a mistake. That's my bag you've got in your hand.'

Brackley smiled tolerantly.

'I'm afraid you've made a mistake yourself, ma'am,' he said. 'You've got your own bag there. You see how alike they are.'

'But I'm *positive*!' the old lady shrieked. She was doing her stuff magnificently, as if she had been coached for the part. 'It was right above my head and you took it. That's my bag you've got. I'd know it anywhere.'

Just as he had hoped, the form of a railway policeman loomed magnificently onto the scene.

'What's going on here?' he asked.

The lady drew breath to speak, but Brackley got in first. He was not going to lose the opportunity he had worked for.

'This lady seems to think I've stolen her bag, officer,' he said. 'I've done nothing of the sort. I'm a perfectly respectable person. My name is Walton, and I'm employed by Mallard's, the London jewellers. I've my business card here if you'd like to see it, and—'

'That'll do, sir, that'll do,' said the constable good-humouredly. 'Nobody's said anything about stealing yet.'

'Of course not,' the lady put in. 'It's a mistake, that's what I keep telling him. But I want my bag, all the same.'

'Quite so, madam.' The officer was enjoying himself hugely. 'Now let's have a look at them.' He laid them side by side upon the platform. 'They are alike, aren't they? No labels, no marks. You careless people! That's the way luggage gets lost, and then it's all blamed onto the railways. What do you say, Mister—'

'Walton is the name.'

'Have you any objection to my opening one of these? That will settle it once for all.'

47

'Not the smallest.'

'And you, madam?'

'Not at all.'

'Here goes, then.'

He took Walton's suitcase, put it upon a bench and unfastened the catch. The lid opened and the pitiless glare of the station lights illuminated what it held. They shone down upon the myriad facets of a mass of jewellery, hastily crammed together, and on top of all a rubber-handled cosh, its tip hideous with a congealed mass of blood and hair — white hair, the hair of old Nicholas Mallard, who even now was lying huddled beneath his counter in Fentiman Street where Walton had left him.

The Manor House Mystery

J. S. Fletcher

1. Misadventure — or Murder?

In a private sitting room of an old-fashioned country-town hotel, a man sat at a writing desk absent-mindedly drawing unmeaning scrawls on a blotting pad. On the table in the centre of the room lay the remains of the last course of a simple dinner; he himself had almost forgotten that he had eaten any dinner. In fact, he had left untouched most of what he had last taken on his plate — in the middle of a spoonful of apple tart he had got up from his chair to walk up and down the room, thinking, speculating, racking his brain; just as abstractedly he had sat down at the desk, to lay hand on a pen, and begin to scribble lines and curves. He went on scribbling lines and curves and circles and various hiero-glyphics, until an old waiter came in and laid the evening newspaper at his side. He started then and looked up, and the waiter glanced at the table.

'You can clear away,' said the absent-minded man. 'I've finished.'

He remained where he was until the table had been cleared and he was once more alone; then he turned his chair to the fire, put his slippered feet on the fender, and picked up the paper. It was a small, four-page sheet, printed at the county town twenty miles away, and it contained little news which had not already appeared in the morning journals. The man turned it over with listless indifference, until his eye lighted on a paragraph, headed 'The Flamstock Mystery'. The indifference went out of his face then; he lifted the folded sheet nearer and read with eagerness.

The mystery attending the death of Mr Septimus Walshawe, JP, of Flamstock, remains still unsolved. That this much-respected townsman and magistrate died of poisoning there is no doubt. It is inconceivable that Mr Walshawe took his own life; no one who was familiar with him could believe for a moment that a man of his cheery temperament, his optimistic character, and his interest in life could ever terminate a useful and fully occupied existence by suicide. Nor is there any evidence that Mr Walshawe took poison by misadventure. There is a growing feeling in Flamstock that the deceased gentleman was – to put it in plain language – murdered, but, although the services of a noted expert in criminal detection have been employed in this case, nothing, we understand, has so far transpired which is likely to lead to the detection of the cowardly – and clever – murderer.

The reader threw the newspaper aside with a smile. He was the noted expert in criminal detection to whom the paragraph referred, and, after several days' investigation of the Walshawe case, he was not quite so certain about the facts which appertained to it as the writer of the paragraph appeared to be. All that he was actually certain about was that he was very much puzzled. He had done a good deal of thinking during the last few days; he knew that a lot of thinking was still to be done. And, realising that there was no likelihood of his thinking of anything else that evening, he lighted a cigar, and settling himself comfortably before the dancing flames, fell to representing the case to his own judgement for perhaps the hundredth time.

This was how the case stood. Mr Septimus Walshawe, a gentleman of about sixty years of age at the time of his sudden death, had lived in Flamstock, a small country town, for twenty-five years. He rented the Manor House, a quaint old mansion at the top of the High Street. He was a man of considerable means, and a bachelor. His tastes were literary and antiquarian. He was the possessor of a notable library; he collected old china, old silver; he had a small but valuable museum of antiquities. He was never so happy as when he was busied about his books and his curiosities, but he was by no means a recluse. From the time of his coming to Flamstock he took a good deal of interest in the life of the town.

He had served on its town council; he had been mayor; he had founded a literary and philosophical institute, and once a year he lectured to its members on some subject of importance. Also, he was a magistrate, and he never failed in his attendance at petty sessions or quarter sessions. In short, he was a feature of the town; everybody knew him; his face and figure was as familiar in High Street as the tower of the old church, or the queer figures which ornamented the town-hall clock.

So much for Mr Walshawe's public life. His private life appeared to have been a very quiet one. His household consisted of a housekeeper, a cook, three female servants, and a boy in buttons; he also employed two gardeners and a groom-coachman, who drove his one equipage, an old-fashioned landau.

He seemed to have no near relations – in fact, the only relation who ever came to see him was a niece, married far away in the North of England, who visited Flamstock for a week or two every year, and for the last few years had brought her two small children with her. It was understood by those Flamstockians who were admitted to Mr Walshawe's confidence that this lady would inherit all he had. And she had inherited it now that he was dead, and it was by her express desire and on her instructions that the New Scotland Yard man who toasted his feet at the fire of his private parlour in the Bull and Bucket had come down to Flamstock to find out the truth about the mystery which surrounded her uncle's death.

That Mr Walshawe's death had taken place under mysterious circumstances there was no doubt. He was found dead in bed at noon on the tenth day of November on a Thursday. The detective had no need to refer to his memoranda for these precise facts as regards Mr Walshawe's doings for some days previous to the day of his death.

Nothing had occurred which could be taken as presaging his decease; he had shown no sign of illness, had made no complaint of any feeling of illness. In fact, he had been rather more than usually active that week.

On the Monday evening he had delivered his annual lecture at the institute; on the Tuesday he had sat on the bench at the town hall from eleven in the morning till five in the afternoon; on the Wednesday he had lunched at Sir Anthony Cleeke's house, just outside the town; that evening he had entertained a few friends to dinner, one or two of whom had stayed rather late.

The fact that they had stayed rather late had relieved Mrs Whiteside, the housekeeper, of any fear when Mr Walshawe did not come down to breakfast at his usual hour next morning. She knew that he had not gone to bed until quite two o'clock.

When breakfast time had been passed by two hours, however, she went to call him, and, getting no answer, walked into his room to find him asleep, but looking so strange and breathing so uneasily that she had become alarmed and sent at once for medical help.

There was delay in getting that. Dr Thorney, Mr Walshawe's medical attendant, was away from home, and his assistant had gone into the country on a round of visits. Consequently an hour elapsed before medical help was brought to his bedside. And when it arrived Mr Walshawe was dead.

In the opinion of the coroner this was decidedly a case for a post-mortem examination, and it was immediately carried out. Its results went to prove that Mr Walshawe had died from veronal poisoning. Thereupon the mystery began.

It was not known to any member of his household that he ever took such things. There was no trace of such things in the house. His private apartments were searched from top to bottom; his desks, his drawers, every receptacle, every nook and cranny where drugs could have been concealed, were scrupulously examined. Nothing was found.

Nor could anybody be found who had ever sold veronal or any similar drug to Mr Walshawe. There were three chemists in Flamstock; none of them had ever known him as a customer for any drug of that sort. Advertisements asking for information on this point were inserted first in the local papers of the neighbouring towns, then in the London newspapers. Had any chemist ever sent veronal to Mr Walshawe by post?

There was no reply to these advertisements. Of course, as plenty of people were quick to point out, Mr Walshawe could have purchased veronal when he was away from the town.

But, as a matter of fact, he had not been away from Flamstock for well over a year. And, in addition to that, those who knew him best and most intimately agreed that he was given to boasting of his general robust health, his good appetite, and, above everything, his power of sleeping. He was the last man in the world, said they, to have need of sleeping draughts; he had been heard to say, a thousand times, that he slept like a top from eleven o'clock until seven. He had said so, Sir Anthony Cleeke remembered, only the day before he was found dead.

It was inconceivable that he should have taken veronal in a sufficient quantity to kill him. Yet the fact remained that he had died from veronal poisoning, and must have taken a considerable dose.

When the man from New Scotland Yard came on the scene, brought there by Mr Walshawe's niece, he had at first come to an immediate conclusion that the dead man had taken the veronal himself. He had had his own reasons, he said, for taking the drug, and being – possibly or probably – unaccustomed to it, he had taken too much.

But he was faced with the fact that no trace of Mr Walshawe ever having bought or possessed such a drug could be found. He was also faced with the general habits and tone of the dead man. He was further having it impressed upon him, day by day, that Mr Walshawe's niece was sure, certain, convinced that somebody had administered the veronal to her uncle in order to do him to death.

She pointed out that there was nothing to show that he was likely to take a sleeping draught; certainly nothing to indicate that he was tired of life. Tired of life, indeed! Why, he was just then full of spirits, full of interests. He was looking forward to attending, on the very day on which he died, a sale by auction at a neighbouring country house, where there were certain antiquities and objects of art which he ardently desired to possess.

He had been talking of them when he lunched at Sir Anthony Cleeke's; he talked of them at his own dinner party in the evening. No – no; nothing would persuade her that her uncle had done anything to bring about his own death. Nothing!

'Misadventure?' suggested the detective.

'No misadventure!' retorted Mr Walshawe's niece. 'My uncle was murdered. It is your place to find out who murdered him.'

This was the problem which vexed the mind of the detective as he sat musing and reflecting in his quiet room at the Bull and Bucket. It seemed to him that he was doing little good. He had been in Flamstock nearly a fortnight, pursuing all sorts of enquiries, following up all manner of suggestions, and he was no nearer any solution of the mystery. Nevertheless, he knew what he wanted. And he muttered a word unconsciously.

'Motive!' he said. 'Motive! Motive!'

A tap came at the door, and the old waiter put his head into the room.

'Mr Peasegood to see you, sir,' he said.

The detective, with the alacrity of a man who is relieved at the prospect of exchanging ideas with a fellow creature, rose.

'Show Mr Peasegood in, William,' he answered.

2. The Legal Visitor

The man who came into the room, contenting himself with a nod of greeting until the waiter had gone away, was known to the detective as Mr Septimus Walshawe's solicitor. He had already had several interviews with him, and they had discussed the details of the case until it seemed as if they had covered every inch of the debatable ground. Yet it now appeared to him that Mr Peasegood had something new to communicate; there was the suggestion of news in his face, and the detective wheeled an easy chair to the hearth with an eagerness which really meant that he was anxious to know what his visitor had to say.

'Good evening, Mr Peasegood,' he said. 'Glad to see you. Can I offer you anything now – a drink, a cigar?'

Mr Peasegood was slowly drawing off his gloves, which he deposited carefully within his hat. He also divested himself of his overcoat, and, having run his fingers over his smooth hair, he dropped into the seat and smiled.

'Not just now, Mr Marshford,' he answered. 'Perhaps a little later. Business first, eh?'

'There is business, then!' exclaimed the detective. 'Ah! Something to do with the case, of course?'

'Something to do with the case, of course,' repeated Mr Peasegood, blandly. 'Very much to do with the case.'

Marshford threw his cigar into the fire and, leaning forward in his chair, looked fixedly at his visitor.

'Yes?' he said.

'You are aware,' continued Peasegood, 'of the tenor of Mr Walshawe's will, which was executed by myself some years ago?'

'Yes, yes,' replied Marshford; 'of course. That is, I know what you told me – that, with the exception of a few trifling legacies, everything was left to the niece, Mrs Carstone?'

'Just so,' assented Peasegood. 'It is ten years since I drew up that will. I have been under the impression that it was Walshawe's last word as to the disposition of his property.'

The detective started.

'And – wasn't it?' he asked eagerly.

Peasegood smiled in an odd fashion.

'Another will – a later will – has come to light,' he replied. He looked narrowly at the detective, and he smiled again. 'It is a perfectly good will,' he added; 'and, of course, it upsets the other.'

'Bless me!' said Marshford. 'I'm sorry to hear it – for Mrs Carstone's sake.'

Peasegood laughed.

'Oh, it doesn't make any great amount of difference to Mrs Carstone!' he remarked. 'Oh, no! But it may make a considerable difference to somebody else in a way which that somebody else won't quite appreciate; a very considerable difference.'

Marshford looked an enquiry. He was eager with inquisitiveness, but he recognised that Peasegood was one of those men who will tell a story in their own way, and he waited.

'This is how it is,' continued Peasegood after a pause; 'and you're the first person I've spoken to about it. This afternoon, just as I was about to leave my office for the day, Mrs Whiteside called on me.'

'Walshawe's housekeeper!' exclaimed Marshford.

'Walshawe's housekeeper – exactly. She requested an interview. Her manner was mysterious. She was some time in coming to a point – I had to ask her, at last, what she really wanted. Eventually she told me that not many months before his death Mr Walshawe made a new will, and entrusted it to her keeping.'

The detective whistled.

'Just so,' continued Peasegood. 'I, too, felt inclined to whistle. Instead, I asked to see the will she spoke of. She produced it. I read it hastily. It is a perfectly good will; nothing can upset it. Or, rather, there's only one thing that might upset it – we'll talk of what that is later. But – to give you particulars of it – it was made on the twenty-fourth of last May; it was written out by Walshawe himself on a sheet of foolscap; it is duly and properly signed and witnessed. Quite a good will.'

'And its provisions?' asked Marshford.

'Simple – very!' replied Peasegood. 'It appoints the same executors – myself and Mr John Entwhistle. Mrs Carstone is left the residue of everything – real and personal estate – as before. The trifling legacies are as before. But a sum of ten thousand pounds is left to Jane Whiteside, and a like sum to her son Richard.'

Peasegood paused and laughed a little.

'That's the difference,' he said, 'a little difference of twenty thousand pounds. I said it would make no difference to Mrs Carstone. It doesn't. Walshawe, first and last, died worth a quarter of a million. Mrs Carstone can easily afford to drop twenty thousand. Twenty thousand is nothing to her. But ten thousand is a lot to Mrs Whiteside – and to her son.'

'To anybody but wealthy people!' exclaimed the detective. 'Um! Well, that's news, Mr Peasegood. But – do you think it has any bearing on the mystery of Walshawe's death?'

Peasegood's eyes and mouth became inscrutable for a minute. Then he smiled.

'You asked me if I'd take anything,' he said. 'I'll take a little whisky, and I'll smoke a cigar. Then – I'll tell you something.'

His face became inscrutable again, and remained so until Marshford had summoned the waiter and his demands for refreshment had been supplied, and he kept silence until he had smoked a good inch of his cigar. When he turned to the detective again it was with a smile that seemed to suggest much.

'I dare say you're as well aware as I am that – especially in professions like yours and mine – men who are practised in deducing one thing from another are apt to think pretty sharply at times,' he said. 'I thought with unusual sharpness when Mrs Whiteside revealed the existence of this will and I'd convinced myself that it would stand. Or, rather, I didn't so much think as remember. I remembered – that's the word – remembered.'

'Remembered – what?' asked Marshford.

Peasegood bent forward with a sidelong glance at the door, and he tapped the detective's knee.

'I remembered two very striking facts – striking in connection with what we know,' he replied, in a whisper. 'First that Jane Whiteside's son, her co-beneficiary, is a chemist in London; second, that he was in Flamstock during the evening and night immediately preceding Walshawe's death. That's what I remembered.'

Marshford opened his eyes to their widest extent. Once more he whistled.

'Whew!' he exclaimed, supplementing the whistle. 'That's – gad, I don't know what that isn't, or is! Anyway, it's news of rare significance.'

'Some people,' observed Peasegood, calmly, 'some people would call it news of sinister significance. It's news that's worth thinking about, anyway. I,' he continued, smiling grimly, 'I have been thinking about it ever since I remembered it.'

'What have you thought?' asked Marshford.

'Nothing that's very clear yet,' replied the solicitor. 'But you may be sure that Mrs Whiteside had long since told her son of the will which she kept locked up in her private repository for such things. He'd no doubt seen it. And a man will dare much for ten thousand pounds.'

'You think he – or he and his mother between them – administered the stuff to Walshawe?' suggested the detective.

'I think,' answered Peasegood deliberately; 'I think that when a man dies as suddenly as Walshawe did, when it's found that he was poisoned, when it's discovered that two people benefit by his death to the extent of twenty thousand pounds, to be paid to them in cash and unconditionally soon after his decease, and when one of these persons is a man acquainted with drugs and their properties – why, then, it's high time that some enquiry should be made.'

'Did you say as much to Mrs Whiteside?' asked Marshford.

'No, I didn't,' replied the solicitor. 'All that I said to Mrs Whiteside was – to ask her why she didn't bring forward this will at once. She replied that she didn't know that there was any occasion for hurry, and that she'd thought she'd wait until things had got settled down a bit.'

The detective reflected in silence for a while.

'What about her manner?' he suddenly asked. 'You'd have thought – good heavens! – why, if they're guilty, you'd have thought they'd be afraid to bring that will forward. They can't be – fools?'

'Apart from her mysterious way of introducing the subject, the woman's manner was calm enough,' answered Peasegood. 'And, as to their being fools, you've got to remember this – the *onus probandi* rests on us if we accuse them. We've got to prove – prove, mind you! – that they, or one of them, poisoned Walshawe, I repeat – prove!'

'The man may be the guilty party, his mother may be perfectly innocent,' remarked Marshford.

'And the mother may be the guilty party, and the son as innocent as you are,' said Peasegood.

Marshford nodded.

'Anyway, there's a motive,' he said. 'But I can see certain things that are in their favour. And the first is – since the son's a chemist, his knowledge would surely show him a cleverer way of getting rid of Walshawe than that. Considering that he's a chemist, and, of course, supposing that he's guilty, it was clumsy – clumsy.'

'I'm not so sure,' replied Peasegood. 'You've got to remember this – good sleeper as Walshawe boasted himself to be, there's nobody can prove that he didn't take drugs at times. For instance, that particular night he'd been giving a dinner party, he sat up, to my knowledge – I was one of his guests – until quite two o'clock. He may have said to himself, as on many similar occasions, "I'm a bit excited. I'll take something to make me sleep," and he may have taken this stuff. You can't prove that he hadn't it by him, any more than you can prove that these people – or one of them – contrived to administer it to him. All you can say is this: Walshawe undoubtedly died of veronal poisoning. There is nothing to show that he ever took veronal. Jane Whiteside and Richard Whiteside benefit by his death to the extent of twenty thousand pounds. They had the opportunity of administering—'

'For that matter,' said Marshford suddenly, 'Jane Whiteside had abundant opportunities – daily opportunities. Why choose that particular night?'

Peasegood got up and began to put on his coat.

'I said, to begin with, that Richard may be the sole guilty party,' he answered. 'He was in Flamstock that night. He came by the six train that Wednesday evening; he left at eight next morning, having spent the night at the Manor House.

And it seems to me that the first thing to do is to find out if Richard Whiteside is in particular need of – his legacy, eh?'

'Just so – just so,' agreed Marshford. 'Leave that to me. I shall want his address.'

Peasegood laid a slip of paper on the table.

'That's his address,' he said. 'Be cautious, Marshford. Well, I'm going.'

The detective accompanied his visitor downstairs. In the hall, a little middle-aged, blue-spectacled man, who carried a bag and a travelling rug, was booking a room at the office window. And when the detective came back from the door, after saying goodnight to Peasegood, the landlady called to him, glancing at the new arrival.

'Here's a gentleman asking for you, Mr Marshford,' she said.

The little blue-spectacled man made a bow, and presented the detective with a card.

'My name and address, sir,' he said politely, in a sharp, business-like fashion. 'Can I have a few words with you?'

Marshford looked at the card, and read:

'William W. Williams, MPS, Dispensing and Family Chemist, The Pharmacy, Llandinas.'

'Come this way, Mr Williams,' responded Marshford.

And as he led his second caller up the stairs, he said to himself that the evening was certainly yielding fruit. For he had no doubt whatever that Mr William W. Williams had come to tell him something about the Walshawe case.

3. The Scientific Visitor

Once within the private sitting room the caller unwound the shawl and comforter in which he was swathed, and took off a heavy travelling overcoat that lay beneath them. He then presented himself as a little, spare man of active frame and movements. What Marshford could see of his eyes beneath his spectacles, and his mouth beneath his beard and moustache, seemed to show that his mind was as active as his body.

He bustled into the chair which Peasegood had just vacated, accepted the detective's offer of a drink with ready cordiality, and, having expressed his thanks in a set phrase, clapped his hands on his knees and looked searchingly at his host.

'I have come a long way to see you, Mr Marshford,' he said. 'Yes, indeed, a long way I have come, sir.'

'That shows that you want to see me on important business, Mr Williams,' observed Marshford. 'I gather that, of course.'

'Important business, sir; oh, yes, indeed! Of the first importance, in my opinion, Mr Marshford,' replied the visitor. He cleared his throat, as if he meant to indulge in a lengthy speech. 'I have read what has been in the papers, sir, about Mr Septimus Walshawe,' he began. 'I gathered from the papers that you are in charge of that case?'

'I am,' said Marshford. 'And if you can throw any light on it, I shall be much obliged to you.'

Williams again cleared his throat.

'I can, sir,' he answered. 'Yes, indeed I can. I knew the late Mr Septimus Walshawe, sir, though I have not set eyes on him for twenty-five years. Mr Walshawe, sir, used to live in Llandinas, and though I have not seen Mr Walshawe since he left − five-and-twenty years ago − I know something about him which, as I gather from the papers, nobody here in Flamstock knows, and you do not know, either. Yes, indeed!'

'Yes?' said Marshford. 'What?'

Williams drew his chair close to the detective's. He wagged his head with a knowing air.

'This, sir,' he said. 'The late Septimus Walshawe was a victim of drugs – or, rather, of one drug. Of one drug, Mr Marshford.'

'What drug?' asked Marshford quietly.

Williams slapped his knees, put his face close to the detective's and rapped out one word.

'Opium!' he said. 'Opium!'

Marshford stared silently at his visitor for a minute or two. Here, indeed, was a revelation which he had not expected – a revelation which might mean a great deal.

'You're quite sure of what you allege?' he asked at last.

'Allege!' exclaimed the chemist, with a laugh. 'I know! Oh, yes, indeed, Mr Marshford! As if I should come all this way, whatever, to talk about something that I wasn't sure of! Oh, yes; I know, sir!'

'What do you know?' said Marshford.

'I know this,' replied Williams. 'Mr Walshawe lived in Llandinas – at a house called Plas Newydd, Mr Marshford – for five years before he came to live here. Soon after he came into Llandinas, he came to my shop for opium. He told me that he had become accustomed to taking it at times for a certain internal disorder which he had contracted while abroad. I made it up for him in five-grain pills. He had so many a month, and as time went on he began to increase his doses. But when he left our neighbourhood he was not taking so much — not nearly so much — as he did later on.'

'How,' asked Marshford, 'how do you know what he took later on?'

The chemist smiled slyly.

'How do I know indeed?' he said. 'Because I have sent him his opium pills to his house here in Flamstock ever since he came here. Yes, indeed; five-and-twenty years I have sent them, once a month. And he needed more and more a month every year. That man, sir, was a victim to the opium habit.'

'You sent him a supply of opium pills regularly?' asked Marshford.

'Once a month I sent them, yes,' replied Williams. 'In a neat box, sir, sealed. Oh, yes; for five-and-twenty years, Mr Marshford!'

'I thought,' remarked Marshford, reflectively, 'that a confirmed opium-taker showed marked signs of the vice?'

'Not always, sir — not always! He wouldn't,' said Williams. 'He was a fresh-coloured, lively-looking man when I knew him, and was to the end, judging from the accounts I've read in the papers. No, sir; I don't think he would show the usual signs much.'

'You don't think that anybody else would detect it?' suggested Marshford.

Williams looked round him, and sank his voice to a whisper.

'I think that somebody here did detect it — was well aware of it,' he answered. 'Yes, indeed, I do, Mr Marshford — oh, yes!'

'Who?' asked Marshford bluntly.

'Whoever poisoned him,' replied the chemist with another sly smile. 'Yes, sir – whoever poisoned him.'

Marshford considered this suggestion awhile. It was some time before he spoke; meanwhile his visitor sat tapping his knees and watching him.

'Look here, Mr Williams,' said the detective at last. 'You've got a theory, and you've come here to tell me what it is. I'm much obliged to you. And now – what is it?'

Williams cleared his throat with one of his sharp, dry coughs.

'This, sir,' he said. 'It seems certain that somebody wanted to get Walshawe out of the way. That somebody knew that he took opium in the shape of pills – probably knew how many he took, and the chemical value of the pills, and made the veronal up to resemble the pills – so closely, indeed, that Walshawe didn't know they weren't opium pills. Yes, indeed!'

'That argues a certain amount of chemical knowledge, Mr Williams,' said Marshford, 'I mean on the part of the poisoner.'

'Oh, it does!' agreed Williams. 'Or it argues that the poisoner knew where to get veronal made up in the form and of the strength he wanted. Oh, yes!'

'That's your theory?' said Marshford.

'That's my theory, sir,' answered the chemist. 'I formed that theory as soon as I read the case in the papers. And having business in London tomorrow I took this place on my way so that I could tell you what I thought. And I venture to predict, sir, that if you ever do get to the bottom of this mystery, you'll find that theory to be correct. Yes, indeed! You don't know of anything that fits in with it, I suppose?'

'I may tell you something about that later, Mr Williams,' replied Marshford. 'I suppose you are going to stay the night here?'

The chemist rose and began to gather together his belongings.

'I am, sir,' he said. 'I am now about to take some much-needed refreshment, and then I am going to bed – I have had a long journey, whatever. I shall have the pleasure of seeing you in the morning, Mr Marshford?'

'Yes, that's it – see me in the morning,' replied Marshford. 'I'm going to think over what you've told me.'

He sat for some time after the chemist had gone away, thinking steadily on the news just given to him. He was beginning to see a clear line now as regards the administration of the veronal, and it certainly seemed to lead to a strong suggestion of the guilt of the Whitesides, mother and son – or, at any rate, one or other of them. It might be that both were concerned; it might be that only the son was concerned. And it might be that the son was innocent and the mother guilty.

'Anyhow,' he murmured, as he drew up a chair to the writing desk, 'the first thing to do is to find out all about the son, and I'll set Chivvins onto that at once.'

But he had scarcely written a line of his letter when the old waiter put his grey head inside the door again and announced the third visitor of the evening.

4. The Imaginative Visitor

'Mr Pitt-Carnaby, sir,' said the waiter, mouthing the double-barrelled name with a reverence which showed Marshford that this latest caller was a person of importance. He bowed the visitor in and moved across the room on pretence of mending the fire. 'Followed me straight in, sir — wouldn't wait,' he whispered to the detective as he passed him.

Marshford looked up from his writing and recognised an elderly gentleman whom he had once or twice seen in the streets of Flamstock and who was chiefly remarkable for the fact that he always wore a knickerbocker suit and a Scotch cap with ribbons depending from its hinder end. He was a bearded and spectacled gentleman. Marshford, on the rare occasions on which he had seen him, had set him down as being a little eccentric. All the same Mr Pitt-Carnaby looked business-like enough as he took the chair which had already been twice occupied that evening.

'Allow me to introduce myself,' said the third visitor. 'I am Mr Pitt-Carnaby, of the Hollies. I have come to speak to you about Mr Walshawe's mysterious death. Mr Walshawe was one of my colleagues on the magisterial bench; he was also a personal friend of mine. We had many tastes in common — we were, for instance, both collectors of antiquities. Naturally, I have thought and reflected a great deal on the circumstances of his sudden decease.'

'I should be very glad of any information, sir,' replied Marshford, almost mechanically. He was not greatly disposed to listen to any further theorisings that night, and he wanted to write his letter to Chivvins. 'Is there something you can tell?' he asked.

Mr Pitt-Carnaby smiled.

'That is a very definite question,' he answered. 'Perhaps I can't reply to it quite so definitely. However, I will say what

I came to say. Has it ever struck you, in the exercise of your calling, that imagination is a very valuable asset?'

Marshford was not quite clear as to his visitor's meaning, and he said so.

'Some people,' continued Mr Pitt-Carnaby, 'bring science – in some shape or other – to bear on these things; I believe that imagination is a surer thing, eh?'

Marshford began to fear that he was in for a very long dissertation from an obvious crank. Nevertheless, it was impossible to get rid of Mr Pitt-Carnaby in summary fashion.

'I suppose you have some theory, sir?' he said, thinking it best to put a direct question.

But the visitor was evidently not the sort of man to be forced into answering direct questions.

'I have allowed my imagination to play round the closing hours of my unfortunate friend's life,' he said. 'Perhaps the result is a theory, though I won't call it so. Instead, I will invite your attention to a few facts. And please to understand that I am not going to mention any names. If I make suggestions, I shall leave you to follow them up.'

Marshford's face lightened; suggestions and facts – especially facts – were things with which he could deal. He left the mantelpiece, against which he had been leaning, and took a chair close to his visitor. Mr Pitt-Carnaby noticed the sudden revival of interest and smiled.

'Very well!' he said. 'The late Mr Walshawe was, like myself, a collector of books, curiosities and antiquities. On the evening before his death he entertained some friends – myself among them – at dinner. Our conversation during the evening turned very largely on a sale by auction which was

to be held next day at a certain country house in this neighbourhood. Many interesting articles were to be offered; the
late tenant of the house in question had been a great collector.
Among those articles was a jar, fashioned of malachite, which,
as you may or may not know, Mr Marshford, is a mineral
scientifically known as basic cupric carbonate. This jar was
of the finer quality of malachite – the malachite found in a
certain district in Siberia, which is used in the manufacture
of mosaics and ornaments. Also, it has a well-authenticated
history – it had once belonged to Peter the Great of Russia,
and it was given by him, during his stay in England in 1698,
to an ancestor of the gentleman whose effects were being
disposed of. Mr Walshawe was very anxious to acquire
this malachite jar. He had a collection of articles which had
belonged to Tsars and Tsarinas of Russia during the past two
centuries, and he wished to add this to it. Concentrate your
attention, then, Mr Marshford, on the fact that on the evening
before his death Mr Walshawe's mind was fixed on buying a
certain malachite jar which was to be offered for sale nearly
twenty miles away at about one o'clock next day.'

Marshford nodded silently. He was beginning to think
that something might come out of this. And Mr Pitt-Carnaby
saw his increasing interest, and went on with his story.

'I repeat,' he said, 'for it is a highly important point, that
Mr Walshawe was absolutely determined to buy this antique.
At dinner that night he talked of it a great deal; he said what
figure he would go to – a heavy one. He anticipated a certain
amount of opposition, for the jar was famous, and there were
likely to be competitors from London, and even from Paris.
However, Mr Walshawe was, as you know, a man of very

large means, and he meant to outbid anybody and everybody. When I left him, a good deal after midnight, he was still gloating over his determination to carry home the malachite jar in triumph from the sale.'

'And he never went to the sale,' remarked Marshford reflectively.

'He never went to the sale – true!' replied Mr Pitt-Carnaby. 'We know, of course, that when that sale began, my unfortunate friend was dead. But I went to the sale, as also did several of my fellow guests of the previous evening. We expected to meet Mr Walshawe there, but he never arrived. One o'clock came – he was still absent. At a quarter past one the famous malachite jar was put up – Mr Walshawe was not there to bid for it. There were many competitors – there were competitors from London and from Paris, as we had thought likely. The bidding began at five hundred guineas and advanced to two thousand guineas, at which sum the malachite jar was knocked down.'

'To whom?' asked Marshford, eagerly.

Mr Pitt-Carnaby rose, and picked up his Scotch cap, his stout stick, and his hand-knitted gloves.

'I said I should mention no names,' he said with a smile, 'but one name I must mention. The malachite jar was sold for two thousand guineas to John Pethington, the house and estate agent in our High Street. Of course, Pethington bought for somebody else. Well, I must now say goodnight, Mr Marshford.'

'But,' exclaimed Marshford, surprised at this sudden termination of the visit, 'but – what do you expect me to do? What—'

Mr Pitt-Carnaby wandered towards the door.

'Oh, what you please!' he answered. 'Of course, if I were in your case, I should find out from Pethington the name of the person for whom he bought the malachite jar.'

'And then?' asked Marshford.

Mr Pitt-Carnaby laid his hand on the door and turned with a sharp look.

'Then?' he said. 'Then you will have the name of the man who poisoned Septimus Walshawe!'

5. *The Plain Truth*

Marshford looked at his watch when Mr Pitt-Carnaby had departed. It was close upon ten o'clock. He believed that most people in Flamstock went to bed at ten o'clock; nevertheless, there was a possibility that some did not. Anyway, it would do him no harm to take a stroll up the High Street. And he threw the scarcely begun letter to Chivvins into the fire, and, putting on his ulster and a travelling cap, went out into the night.

There were lights in the windows of Mr Pethington's house, and when Marshford rang the bell, Mr Pethington, a fat-faced, stolid-looking man, answered the summons in person. As the light of his hall lamp fell on Marshford's face Pethington silently moved aside, motioning the detective to enter. When Marshford stepped within, Pethington just as silently showed him into a small room near the door. He turned up a solitary gas jet, and looked at his visitor with the calm interrogation of a man who expects to be asked questions.

'You know me, Mr Pethington, and what my business is?'

said Marshford, in a low voice. 'I can take that for granted, of course?'

Pethington leaned back against his desk, and put his hands in his pockets.

'I don't know what it is at present,' he answered, 'I know what you're after in the town, of course.'

'I want to ask a very simple question,' said Marshford. 'It's one which you'll have to answer sooner or later, and I wish you'd answer it now. For whom did you purchase that malachite jar? You know what I mean.'

Pethington showed no surprise. Instead, he merely nodded, as if he had expected to have this question put to him, and he pulled out his watch, noting the time.

'Instead of asking me to answer that question, Mr Marshford,' he said, 'I wish you'd just step round to the police station.'

Marshford stared at this unexpected reply.

'Why?' he exclaimed.

'Because I think you'll get an answer to it there,' replied Pethington, dropping his watch into his pocket.

The two men exchanged looks. Then Pethington nodded.

'You'll find I'm right,' he said.

Marshford went away from the house without a word. He walked rapidly up the deserted High Street towards the town hall, wondering what this sudden development implied. And suddenly, rounding a corner, and in the full light of a street lamp, he ran into Peasegood.

'I was just coming to you,' said the solicitor. 'Well, the truth's out at last – just got it. Good heavens, what a world this is!'

'What is it?' demanded Marshford. 'You don't mean that somebody's confessed to poisoning Walshawe?'

'That's just what I do mean,' replied Peasegood; 'the last man in the world I should have suspected, too!'

'Who, then?' exclaimed Marshford.

Peasegood took off his hat and wiped his forehead. Then he spoke one word – a name:

'Thorney!'

'What!' said Marshford. 'The doctor?'

'The doctor!' repeated Peasegood. 'He's just told the inspector and me all about it. It was by inadvertence. Dr Thorney, you must know, is an ardent collector of certain things, as Walshawe was. He was bent on having a certain jar of malachite, with a history attached to it, which was to be put up at that sale I told you of. Walshawe was bent on it, too – vowed he'd have it. Thorney – you know that these collectors spare no pains to steal a march on each other – resolved to play a trick on Walshawe. It turned out that Walshawe took opium secretly, in pills – Thorney knew it, and knew where he kept his pills, in a little case on his desk. That night when we all dined there, Thorney got into Walshawe's study by himself, took the opium pills out of the case, and substituted veronal which he'd made up himself. His idea was to make Walshawe sleep far into the next day, until he was too late for the sale. If things had gone as Thorney intended, Walshawe would have slept until the afternoon and been all right after. But Thorney forgot one very important thing.'

'What?' asked Marshford, eagerly.

'He didn't know how many opium pills Walshawe did, or could, take,' answered the solicitor, 'and so you see

Walshawe took sufficient veronal to poison him. Misadventure, of course, in Thorney's eyes, but—'

He paused, and looked thoughtfully down the long vista of the High Street as the two men turned away together.

'But – what?' asked Marshford.

'I wonder what the judge will tell the jury to call it?' answered Peasegood.

The Man Who Knew How

Dorothy L. Sayers

For perhaps the twentieth time since the train had left Carlisle, Pender glanced up from *Murder at the Manse* and caught the eye of the man opposite.

He frowned a little. It was irritating to be watched so closely, and always with that faint, sardonic smile. It was still more irritating to allow oneself to be so much disturbed by the smile and the scrutiny. Pender wrenched himself back to his book with a determination to concentrate upon the problem of the minister murdered in the library. But the story was of the academic kind that crowds all its exciting incidents into the first chapter, and proceeds thereafter by a long series of deductions to a scientific solution in the last. The thin thread of interest, spun precariously upon the wheel of Pender's reasoning brain, had been snapped. Twice he had to turn back to verify points that he had missed in reading. Then he became aware that his eyes had followed three closely argued pages without conveying anything whatever to his intelligence. He was not thinking about the murdered minister at all – he was becoming more and more actively conscious of the other man's face. A queer face, Pender thought.

There was nothing especially remarkable about the features in themselves; it was their expression that daunted Pender. It was a secret face, the face of one who knew a great deal to other people's disadvantage. The mouth was a little crooked and tightly tucked in at the corners, as though savouring a hidden amusement. The eyes, behind a pair of rimless pince-nez, glittered curiously; but that was possibly due to the light reflected in the glasses. Pender wondered what the man's profession might be. He was dressed in a dark lounge suit, a raincoat and a shabby soft hat; his age was perhaps about forty.

Pender coughed unnecessarily and settled back into his corner, raising the detective story high before his face, barrier-fashion. This was worse than useless. He gained the impression that the man saw through the manoeuvre and was secretly entertained by it. He wanted to fidget, but felt obscurely that his doing so would in some way constitute a victory for the other man. In his self-consciousness he held himself so rigid that attention to his book became a sheer physical impossibility.

There was no stop now before Rugby, and it was unlikely that any passenger would enter from the corridor to break up this disagreeable *solitude à deux*. But something must be done. The silence had lasted so long that any remark, however trivial, would – so Pender felt – burst upon the tense atmosphere with the unnatural clatter of an alarm clock. One could, of course, go out into the corridor and not return, but that would be an acknowledgment of defeat. Pender lowered *Murder at the Manse* and caught the man's eye again.

'Getting tired of it?' asked the man.

'Night journeys are always a bit tedious,' replied Pender, half relieved and half reluctant. 'Would you like a book?'

He took *The Paper-Clip Clue* from his attaché case and held it out hopefully. The other man glanced at the title and shook his head.

'Thanks very much,' he said, 'but I never read detective stories. They're so — inadequate, don't you think so?'

'They are rather lacking in characterisation and human interest, certainly,' said Pender, 'but on a railway journey—'

'I don't mean that,' said the other man. 'I am not concerned with humanity. But all these murderers are so incompetent — they bore me.'

'Oh, I don't know,' replied Pender. 'At any rate they are usually a good deal more imaginative and ingenious than murderers in real life.'

'Than the murderers who are found out in real life, yes,' admitted the other man.

'Even some of those did pretty well before they got pinched,' objected Pender. 'Crippen, for instance; he need never have been caught if he hadn't lost his head and run off to America. George Joseph Smith did away with at least two brides quite successfully before fate and the *News of the World* intervened.'

'Yes,' said the other man, 'but look at the clumsiness of it all; the elaboration, the lies, the paraphernalia. Absolutely unnecessary.'

'Oh, come!' said Pender. 'You can't expect committing a murder and getting away with it to be as simple as shelling peas.'

'Ah!' said the other man. 'You think that, do you?'

Pender waited for him to elaborate this remark, but nothing came of it. The man leaned back and smiled in his secret way at the roof of the carriage; he appeared to think the conversation not worth going on with. Pender, taking up his book again, found himself attracted by his companion's hands. They were white and surprisingly long in the fingers. He watched them gently tapping upon their owner's knee – then resolutely turned a page – then put the book down once more and said:

'Well, if it's so easy, how would *you* set about committing a murder?'

'I?' repeated the man. The light on his glasses made his eyes quite blank to Pender, but his voice sounded gently amused. 'That's different; *I* should not have to think twice about it.'

'Why not?'

'Because I happen to know how to do it.'

'Do you indeed?' muttered Pender, rebelliously.

'Oh, yes; there's nothing in it.'

'How can you be sure? You haven't tried, I suppose?'

'It isn't a case of trying,' said the man. 'There's nothing tentative about my method. That's just the beauty of it.'

'It's easy to say that,' retorted Pender, 'but what *is* this wonderful method?'

'You can't expect me to tell you that, can you?' said the other man, bringing his eyes back to rest on Pender's. 'It might not be safe. You look harmless enough, but who could look more harmless than Crippen? Nobody is fit to be trusted with *absolute* control over other people's lives.'

'Bosh!' exclaimed Pender. 'I shouldn't think of murdering anybody.'

'Oh, yes, you would,' said the other man, 'if you really believed it was safe. So would anybody. Why are all these tremendous artificial barriers built up around murder by the Church and the law? Just because it's everybody's crime, and just as natural as breathing.'

'But that's ridiculous!' cried Pender, warmly.

'You think so, do you? That's what most people would say. But I wouldn't trust 'em. Not with sulphate of thanatol to be bought for twopence at any chemist's.'

'Sulphate of what?' asked Pender sharply.

'Ah! you think I'm giving something away. Well, it's a mixture of that and one or two other things — all equally ordinary and cheap. For ninepence you could make up enough to poison the entire Cabinet — and even you would hardly call that a crime, would you? But of course one wouldn't polish the whole lot off at once; it might look funny if they all died simultaneously in their baths.'

'Why in their baths?'

'That's the way it would take them. It's the action of the hot water that brings on the effect of the stuff, you see. Any time from a few hours to a few days after administration. It's quite a simple chemical reaction and it couldn't possibly be detected by analysis. It would just look like heart failure.'

Pender eyed him uneasily. He did not like the smile; it was not only derisive, it was smug, it was almost — gloating — triumphant! He could not quite put a name to it.

'You know,' pursued the man, thoughtfully pulling a pipe from his pocket and beginning to fill it, 'it is very odd how often one seems to read of people being found dead in their baths. It must be a very common accident. Quite temptingly so. After all, there is a fascination about murder. The thing grows upon one – that is, I imagine it would, you know.'

'Very likely,' said Pender.

'Look at Palmer. Look at Gesina Gottfried. Look at Armstrong. No, I wouldn't trust anybody with that formula – not even a virtuous young man like yourself.'

The long white fingers tamped the tobacco firmly into the bowl and struck a match.

'But how about you?' said Pender, irritated. (Nobody cares to be called a virtuous young man.) 'If nobody is fit to be trusted—'

'I'm not, eh?' replied the man. 'Well, that's true, but it's past praying for now, isn't it? I know the thing and I can't unknow it again. It's unfortunate, but there it is. At any rate you have the comfort of knowing that nothing disagreeable is likely to happen to *me*. Dear me! Rugby already. I get out here. I have a little bit of business to do at Rugby.'

He rose and shook himself, buttoned his raincoat about him and pulled the shabby hat more firmly down above his enigmatic glasses. The train slowed down and stopped. With a brief goodnight and a crooked smile the man stepped on to the platform. Pender watched him stride quickly away into the drizzle beyond the radius of the gas light.

'Dotty or something,' said Pender, oddly relieved. 'Thank goodness, I seem to be going to have the carriage to myself.'

He returned to *Murder at the Manse*, but his attention still kept wandering.

'What was the name of that stuff the fellow talked about?' For the life of him he could not remember.

It was on the following afternoon that Pender saw the news item. He had bought the *Standard* to read at lunch, and the word 'bath' caught his eye; otherwise he would probably have missed the paragraph altogether, for it was only a short one.

WEALTHY MANUFACTURER DIES IN BATH
WIFE'S TRAGIC DISCOVERY

A distressing discovery was made early this morning by Mrs John Brittlesea, wife of the well-known head of Brittlesea's Engineering Works at Rugby. Finding that her husband, whom she had seen alive and well less than an hour previously, did not come down in time for his breakfast, she searched for him in the bathroom, where, on the door being broken down, the engineer was found lying dead in his bath, life having been extinct, according to the medical men, for half an hour. The cause of the death is pronounced to be heart failure. The deceased manufacturer ...'

'That's an odd coincidence,' said Pender. 'At Rugby. I should think my unknown friend would be interested – if he is still there, doing his bit of business. I wonder what his business is, by the way.'

It is a very curious thing how, when once your attention is attracted to any particular set of circumstances, that set

of circumstances seems to haunt you. You get appendicitis: immediately the newspapers are filled with paragraphs
about statesmen suffering from appendicitis and victims
dying of it; you learn that all your acquaintances have had
it, or know friends who have had it, and either died of it,
or recovered from it with more surprising and spectacular
rapidity than yourself; you cannot open a popular magazine
without seeing its cure mentioned as one of the triumphs
of modern surgery, or dip into a scientific treatise without
coming across a comparison of the vermiform appendix in
men and monkeys. Probably these references to appendicitis
are equally frequent at all times, but you only notice them
when your mind is attuned to the subject. At any rate, it was
in this way that Pender accounted to himself for the extraordinary frequency with which people seemed to die in their
baths at this period.

The thing pursued him at every turn. Always the same
sequence of events: the hot bath, the discovery of the corpse,
the inquest; always the same medical opinion: heart failure
following immersion in too-hot water. It began to seem to
Pender that it was scarcely safe to enter a hot bath at all. He
took to making his own bath cooler and cooler every day,
until it almost ceased to be enjoyable.

He skimmed his paper each morning for headlines about
baths before settling down to read the news; and was at once
relieved and vaguely disappointed if a week passed without
a hot-bath tragedy.

One of the sudden deaths that occurred in this way was
that of a young and beautiful woman whose husband, an
analytical chemist, had tried without success to divorce her

a few months previously. The coroner displayed a tendency to suspect foul play, and put the husband through a severe cross examination. There seemed, however, to be no getting behind the doctor's evidence. Pender, brooding fancifully over the improbable possible, wished, as he did every day of the week, that he could remember the name of that drug the man in the train had mentioned.

Then came the excitement in Pender's own neighbourhood. An old Mr Skimmings, who lived alone with a housekeeper in a street just round the corner, was found dead in his bathroom. His heart had never been strong. The housekeeper told the milkman that she had always expected something of the sort to happen, for the old gentleman would always take his bath so hot. Pender went to the inquest.

The housekeeper gave her evidence. Mr Skimmings had been the kindest of employers, and she was heartbroken at losing him. No, she had not been aware that Mr Skimmings had left her a large sum of money, but it was just like his goodness of heart. The verdict was death by misadventure.

Pender, that evening, went out for his usual stroll with the dog. Some feeling of curiosity moved him to go round past the late Mr Skimmings' house. As he loitered by, glancing up at the blank windows, the garden gate opened and a man came out. In the light of a street lamp, Pender recognised him at once.

'Hullo!' he said.

'Oh, it's you, is it?' said the man. 'Viewing the site of the tragedy, eh? What do *you* think about it all?'

'Oh, nothing very much,' said Pender. 'I didn't know him. Odd, our meeting again like this.'

'Yes, isn't it? You live near here, I suppose.'

'Yes,' said Pender; and then wished he hadn't. 'Do you live in these parts too?'

'Me?' said the man. 'Oh, no. I was only here on a little matter of business.'

'Last time we met,' said Pender, 'you had business at Rugby.' They had fallen into step together, and were walking slowly down to the turning Pender had to take in order to reach his house.

'So I had,' agreed the other man. 'My business takes me all over the country. I never know where I may be wanted next.'

'It was while you were at Rugby that old Brittlesea was found dead in his bath, wasn't it?' remarked Pender carelessly.

'Yes. Funny thing, coincidence.' The man glanced up at him sideways through his glittering glasses. 'Left all his money to his wife, didn't he? She's a rich woman now. Good-looking girl – a lot younger than he was.'

They were passing Pender's gate. 'Come in and have a drink,' said Pender, and again immediately regretted the impulse.

The man accepted, and they went into Pender's bachelor study.

'Remarkable lot of these bath deaths there have been lately, haven't there?' observed Pender carelessly, as he splashed soda into the tumblers.

'You think it's remarkable?' said the man, with his usual irritating trick of querying everything that was said to him. 'Well, I don't know. Perhaps it is. But it's always a fairly common accident.'

'I suppose I've been taking more notice on account of that

conversation we had in the train.' Pender laughed, a little self-consciously. 'It just makes me wonder – you know how one does – whether anybody else had happened to hit on that drug you mentioned – what was its name?'

The man ignored the question.

'Oh, I shouldn't think so,' he said. 'I fancy I'm the only person who knows about that. I only stumbled on the thing by accident myself when I was looking for something else. I don't imagine it could have been discovered simultaneously in so many parts of the country. But all these verdicts just show, don't they, what a safe way it would be of getting rid of a person.'

'You're a chemist, then?' asked Pender, catching at the one phrase which seemed to promise information.

'Oh, I'm a bit of everything. Sort of general utility man. I do a good bit of studying on my own, too. You've got one or two interesting books here, I see.'

Pender was flattered. For a man in his position – he had been in a bank until he came into that little bit of money – he felt that he had improved his mind to some purpose, and he knew that his collection of modern first editions would be worth money some day. He went over to the glass-fronted bookcase and pulled out a volume or two to show his visitor.

The man displayed intelligence, and presently joined him in front of the shelves.

'These, I take it, represent your personal tastes?' He took down a volume of Henry James and glanced at the fly leaf. 'That your name? E. Pender?'

Pender admitted that it was. 'You have the advantage of me,' he added.

'Oh! I am one of the great Smith clan,' said the other with a laugh, 'and work for my bread. You seem to be very nicely fixed here.'

Pender explained about the clerkship and the legacy.

'Very nice, isn't it?' said Smith. 'Not married? No. You're one of the lucky ones. Not likely to be needing any sulphate of … any useful drugs in the near future. And you never will, if you stick to what you've got and keep off women and speculation.'

He smiled up sideways at Pender. Now that his hat was off, Pender saw that he had a quantity of closely curled grey hair, which made him look older than he had appeared in the railway carriage.

'No, I shan't be coming to you for assistance yet awhile,' said Pender, laughing. 'Besides, how should I find you if I wanted you?'

'You wouldn't have to,' said Smith. '*I* should find *you*. There's never any difficulty about that.' He grinned, oddly. 'Well, I'd better be getting on. Thank you for your hospitality. I don't expect we shall meet again – but we may, of course. Things work out so queerly, don't they?'

When he had gone, Pender returned to his own armchair. He took up his glass of whisky, which stood there nearly full.

'Funny!' he said to himself. 'I don't remember pouring that out. I suppose I got interested and did it mechanically.' He emptied his glass slowly, thinking about Smith.

What in the world was Smith doing at Skimmings' house?

An odd business altogether. If Skimmings' housekeeper had known about that money … But she had not known, and if she had, how could she have found out about Smith and his sulphate of ... the word had been on the tip of his tongue then.

'You would not need to find me. *I* should find *you*.' What had the man meant by that? But this was ridiculous. Smith was not the devil, presumably. But if he really had this secret – if he liked to put a price upon it – nonsense.

'Business at Rugby – a little bit of business at Skimmings' house.' Oh, absurd!

'Nobody is fit to be trusted. *Absolute* power over another man's life ... it grows on you.'

Lunacy! And, if there was anything in it, the man was mad to tell Pender about it. If Pender chose to speak he could get the fellow hanged. The very existence of Pender would be dangerous.

That whisky!

More and more, thinking it over, Pender became persuaded that he had never poured it out. Smith must have done it while his back was turned. Why that sudden display of interest in the bookshelves? It had had no connection with anything that had gone before. Now Pender came to think of it, it had been a very stiff whisky. Was it imagination, or had there been something about the flavour of it?

A cold sweat broke out on Pender's forehead.

A quarter of an hour later, after a powerful dose of mustard and water, Pender was downstairs again, very cold and shivering, huddling over the fire. He had had a narrow escape – if he had escaped. He did not know how the stuff worked, but he would not take a hot bath again for some days. One never knew.

*

Whether the mustard and water had done the trick in time, or whether the hot bath was an essential part of the treatment, Pender's life was saved for the time being. But he was still uneasy. He kept the front door on the chain and warned his servant to let no strangers into the house.

He ordered two more morning papers and the *News of the World* on Sundays, and kept a careful watch upon their columns. Deaths in baths became an obsession with him. He neglected his first editions and took to attending inquests.

Three weeks later he found himself at Lincoln. A man had died of heart failure in a Turkish bath – a fat man, of sedentary habits. The jury added a rider to their verdict of misadventure, to the effect that the management should exercise a stricter supervision over the bathers and should never permit them to be left unattended in the hot room.

As Pender emerged from the hall he saw ahead of him a shabby hat that seemed familiar. He plunged after it, and caught Mr Smith about to step into a taxi.

'Smith,' he cried, gasping a little. He clutched him fiercely by the shoulder.

'What, you again?' said Smith. 'Taking notes of the case, eh? Can I do anything for you?'

'You devil!' said Pender. 'You're mixed up in this! You tried to kill me the other day.'

'Did I? Why should I do that?'

'You'll swing for this,' shouted Pender menacingly.

A policeman pushed his way through the gathering crowd.

'Here!' said he, 'what's all this about?'

Smith touched his forehead significantly.

'It's all right, officer,' said he. 'The gentleman seems to

think I'm here for no good. Here's my card. The coroner knows me. But he attacked me. You'd better keep an eye on him.'

'That's right,' said a bystander.

'This man tried to kill me,' said Pender.

The policeman nodded.

'Don't you worry about that, sir,' he said. 'You think better of it. The 'eat in there has upset you a bit. All right, *all* right.'

'But I want to charge him,' said Pender.

'I wouldn't do that if I was you,' said the policeman.

'I tell you,' said Pender, 'that this man Smith has been trying to poison me. He's a murderer. He's poisoned scores of people.'

The policeman winked at Smith.

'Best be off, sir,' he said. 'I'll settle this. Now, my lad' – he held Pender firmly by the arms – 'just you keep cool and take it quiet. That gentleman's name ain't Smith nor nothing like it. You've got a bit mixed up like.'

'Well, what is his name?' demanded Pender.

'Never you mind,' replied the constable. 'You leave him alone, or you'll be getting yourself into trouble.'

The taxi had driven away. Pender glanced round at the circle of amused faces and gave in.

'All right, officer,' he said. 'I won't give you any trouble. I'll come round with you to the police station and tell you about it.'

'What do you think o' that one?' asked the inspector of the sergeant when Pender had stumbled out of the station.

'Up the pole an' 'alf-way round the flag, if you ask me,' replied his subordinate. 'Got one o' them ideez fix what they talk about.'

'Hm!' replied the inspector. 'Well, we've got his name and address. Better make a note of 'em. He might turn up again. Poisoning people so as they die in their baths, eh? That's a pretty good 'un. Wonderful how these barmy ones think it all out, isn't it?'

The spring that year was a bad one – cold and foggy. It was March when Pender went down to an inquest at Deptford, but a thick blanket of mist was hanging over the river as though it were November. The cold ate into your bones. As he sat in the dingy little court, peering through the yellow twilight of gas and fog, he could scarcely see the witnesses as they came to the table. Everybody in the place seemed to be coughing. Pender was coughing too. His bones ached, and he felt as though he were about due for a bout of influenza.

Straining his eyes, he thought he recognised a face on the other side of the room, but the smarting fog which penetrated every crack stung and blinded him. He felt in his overcoat pocket, and his hand closed comfortably on something thick and heavy. Ever since that day in Lincoln he had gone about armed for protection. Not a revolver – he was no hand with firearms. A sandbag was much better. He had bought one from an old man wheeling a barrow. It was meant for keeping out draughts from the door – a good, old-fashioned affair.

The inevitable verdict was returned. The spectators began to push their way out. Pender had to hurry now, not to lose sight of his man. He elbowed his way along, muttering apologies. At the door he almost touched the man, but a stout woman intervened. He plunged past her, and she gave a little squeak of indignation. The man in front turned his head, and the light over the door glinted on his glasses.

Pender pulled his hat over his eyes and followed. His shoes had crêpe rubber soles and made no sound on the sticking pavement. The man went on, jogging quietly up one street and down another, and never looking back. The fog was so thick that Pender was forced to keep within a few yards of him. Where was he going? Into the lighted streets? Home by bus or tram? No. He turned off to the left, down a narrow street.

The fog was thicker here. Pender could no longer see his quarry, but he heard the footsteps going on before him at the same even pace. It seemed to him that they were two alone in the world – pursued and pursuer, slayer and avenger. The street began to slope more rapidly. They must be coming out somewhere near the river.

Suddenly the dim shapes of the houses fell away on either side. There was an open space, with a lamp vaguely visible in the middle. The footsteps paused. Pender, silently hurrying after, saw the man standing close beneath the lamp, apparently consulting something in a notebook.

Four steps, and Pender was upon him. He drew the sandbag from his pocket. The man looked up.

'I've got you this time,' said Pender, and struck with all his force.

Pender had been quite right. He did get influenza. It was a week before he was out and about again. The weather had changed, and the air was fresh and sweet. In spite of the weakness left by the malady he felt as though a heavy weight had been lifted from his shoulders. He tottered down to a favourite bookshop of his in the Strand, and picked up a D. H. Lawrence 'first' at a price which he knew to be a bargain. Encouraged by this, he turned into a small chop house, chiefly frequented by Fleet Street men, and ordered a grilled cutlet and a half-tankard of bitter.

Two journalists were seated at the next table.

'Going to poor old Buckley's funeral?' asked one

'Yes,' said the other. 'Poor devil! Fancy his getting sloshed on the head like that. He must have been on his way down to interview the widow of that fellow who died in a bath. It's a rough district. Probably one of Jimmy the Card's crowd had it in for him. He was a great crime reporter – they won't get another like Bill Buckley in a hurry.'

'He was a decent sort, too. Great old sport. No end of a leg-puller. Remember his great stunt about sulphate of thanatol?'

Pender started. *That* was the word that had eluded him for so many months. A curious dizziness came over him and he took a pull at the tankard to steady himself.

'... looking at you as sober as a judge,' the journalist was saying. 'He used to work off that wheeze on poor boobs in railway carriages to see how they'd take it. Would you believe that one chap actually offered him—'

'Hullo!' interrupted his friend. 'That bloke over there has fainted. I thought he was looking a bit white.'

The Ghost's Touch

Fergus Hume

I shall never forget the terrible Christmas I spent at Ring-shaw Grange in the year '93. As an army doctor I have met with strange adventures in far lands, and have seen some gruesome sights in the little wars which are constantly being waged on the frontiers of our empire; but it was reserved for an old country house in Hants to be the scene of the most noteworthy episode in my life. The experience was a painful one, and I hope it may never be repeated; but indeed so ghastly an event is not likely to occur again. If my story reads more like fiction than truth, I can only quote the well-worn saying, of the latter being stranger than the former. Many a time in my wandering life have I proved the truth of this proverb.

The whole affair rose out of the invitation which Frank Ringan sent me to spend Christmas with himself and his cousin Percy at the family seat near Christchurch. At that time I was home on leave from India; and shortly after my arrival I chanced to meet with Percy Ringan in Piccadilly. He was an Australian with whom I had been intimate some years before in Melbourne: a dapper little man with sleek fair hair and a transparent complexion, looking as fragile as a Dresden china image, yet with plenty of pluck and spirits. He suffered from heart disease, and was liable to faint on occasions; yet he fought against his mortal weakness with silent courage, and with certain precautions against over-excitement, he managed to enjoy life fairly well.

Notwithstanding his pronounced effeminacy, and some-what truckling subserviency to rank and high birth, I liked the little man very well for his many good qualities. On the present occasion I was glad to see him, and expressed my pleasure.

'Although I did not expect to see you in England,' said I, after the first greetings had passed.

'I have been in London these nine months, my dear Lascelles,' he said, in his usual mincing way, 'partly by way of a change and partly to see my cousin Frank – who indeed invited me to come over from Australia.'

'Is that the rich cousin you were always speaking about in Melbourne?'

'Yes. But Frank is not rich. I am the wealthy Ringan, but he is the head of the family. You see, Doctor,' continued Percy, taking my arm and pursuing the subject in a conver-sational manner, 'my father, being a younger son, emigrated to Melbourne in the gold-digging days, and made his fortune out there. His brother remained at home on the estates, with very little money to keep up the dignity of the family; so my father helped the head of his house from time to time. Five years ago both my uncle and father died, leaving Frank and me as heirs, the one to the family estate, the other to the Australian wealth. So—'

'So you assist your cousin to keep up the dignity of the family as your father did before you.'

'Well, yes, I do,' admitted Percy, frankly. 'You see, we Ringans think a great deal of our birth and position. So much so, that we have made our wills in one another's favour.'

'How do you mean?'

'Well, if I die Frank inherits my money; and if he dies, I become heir to the Ringan estates. It seems strange that I should tell you all this, Lascelles; but you were so intimate with me in the old days that you can understand my apparent rashness.'

I could not forbear a chuckle at the reason assigned by Percy for his confidence, especially as it was such a weak one. The little man had a tongue like a town-crier, and could no more keep his private affairs to himself than a woman could guard a secret. Besides, I saw very well that with his inherent snobbishness he desired to impress me with the position and antiquity of his family, and with the fact – undoubtedly true – that it ranked among the landed gentry of the kingdom.

However, the weakness, though in bad taste, was harmless enough, and I had no scorn for the confession of it. Still, I felt a trifle bored, as I took little interest in the chronicling of such small beer, and shortly parted from Percy after promising to dine with him the following week.

At this dinner, which took place at the Athenian Club, I met with the head of the Ringan family; or, to put it plainer, with Percy's cousin Frank. Like the Australian he was small and neat, but enjoyed much better health and lacked the effeminacy of the other. Yet on the whole I liked Percy the best, as there was a sly cast about Frank's countenance which I did not relish; and he patronised his colonial cousin in rather an offensive manner.

The latter looked up to his English kinsman with all deference, and would, I am sure, have willingly given his gold to regild the somewhat tarnished escutcheon of the Ringans. Outwardly, the two cousins were so alike as to remind one of Tweedledum and Tweedledee; but after due consideration I decided that Percy was the better-natured and more honourable of the two.

For some reason Frank Ringan seemed desirous of cultivating my acquaintance; and in one way and another I saw a good deal of him during my stay in London. Finally, when I was departing on a visit to some relatives in Norfolk he invited me to spend Christmas at Ringshaw Grange – not, as it afterwards appeared, without an ulterior motive.

'I can take no refusal,' said he, with a heartiness which sat ill on him. 'Percy, as an old friend of yours, has set his heart on my having you down; and – if I may say so – I have set my heart on the same thing.'

'Oh, you really must come, Lascelles,' cried Percy, eagerly. 'We are going to keep Christmas in the real old English fashion. Washington Irving's style, you know: holly, wassail-bowl, games and mistletoe.'

'And perhaps a ghost or so,' finished Frank, laughing, yet with a side glance at his eager little cousin.

'Ah,' said I. 'So your Grange is haunted.'

'I should think so,' said Percy, before his cousin could speak, 'and with a good old Queen Anne ghost. Come down, Doctor, and Frank shall put you in the haunted chamber.'

'No!' cried Frank, with a sharpness which rather surprised me, 'I'll put no one in the Blue Room; the consequences might be fatal. You smile, Lascelles, but I assure you our ghost has been proved to exist!'

'That's a paradox; a ghost can't exist. But the story of your ghost—'

'Is too long to tell now,' said Frank, laughing. 'Come down to the Grange and you'll hear it.'

'Very good,' I replied, rather attracted by the idea of a haunted house, 'you can count upon me for Christmas. But I warn you, Ringan, that I don't believe in spirits. Ghosts went out with gas.'

'Then they must have come in again with electric light,' retorted Frank Ringan, 'for Lady Joan undoubtedly haunts the Grange. I don't mind as it adds distinction to the house.'

'All old families have a ghost,' said Percy, importantly. 'It is very natural when one has ancestors.'

There was no more said on the subject for the time being, but the upshot of this conversation was that I presented myself at Ringshaw Grange two or three days before Christmas. To speak the truth, I came more on Percy's account than my own, as I knew the little man suffered from heart disease, and a sudden shock might prove fatal. If, in the unhealthy atmosphere of an old house, the inmates got talking of ghosts and goblins, it might be that the consequences would be dangerous to so highly strung and delicate a man as Percy Ringan.

For this reason, joined to a sneaking desire to see the ghost, I found myself a guest at Ringshaw Grange. In one way I regret the visit; yet in another I regard it as providential that I was on the spot. Had I been absent the catastrophe might have been greater, although it could scarcely have been more terrible.

Ringshaw Grange was a quaint Elizabethan house, all gables and diamond casements, and oriel windows, and quaint terraces, looking like an illustration out of an old Christmas number. It was embowered in a large park, the trees of which came up almost to the doors, and when I saw it first in the moonlight – for it was by a late train that I came from London – it struck me as the very place for a ghost.

Here was a haunted house of the right quality if ever there was one, and I only hoped when I crossed the threshold that the local spectre would be worthy of its environment. In such an interesting house I did not think to pass a dull Christmas; but – God help me – I did not anticipate so tragic a Yuletide as I spent.

As our host was a bachelor and had no female relative to do the honours of his house the guests were all of the masculine gender. It is true that there was a housekeeper – a distant cousin, I understood – who was rather elderly but very juvenile as to dress and manner. She went by the name of Miss Laura, but no one saw much of her as, otherwise than attending to her duties, she remained mostly in her own rooms.

So our party was composed of young men – none save myself being over the age of thirty, and few being gifted with much intelligence. The talk was mostly of sport, of horse-racing, big-game shooting, and yacht sailing: so that I grew tired at times of these subjects and retired to the library to read and write. The day after I arrived Frank showed me over the house.

It was a wonderful old barrack of a place, with broad passages, twisting interminably like the labyrinth of Daedalus; small bedrooms furnished in an old-fashioned manner; and vast reception apartments with polished floors and painted ceilings. Also there were the customary number of family portraits frowning from the walls; suits of tarnished armour; and ancient tapestries embroidered with grim and ghastly legends of the past.

The old house was crammed with treasures, rare enough to drive an antiquarian crazy; and filled with the flotsam and jetsam of many centuries, mellowed by time into one soft hue, which put them all in keeping with one another. I must say that I was charmed with Ringshaw Grange, and no longer wondered at the pride taken by Percy Ringan in his family and their past glories.

'That's all very well,' said Frank, to whom I remarked as much; 'Percy is rich, and had he this place could keep it up in proper style; but I am as poor as a rat, and unless I can make a rich marriage, or inherit a comfortable legacy, house and furniture, park and timber may all come to the hammer.'

He looked gloomy as he spoke; and, feeling that I had touched on a somewhat delicate matter, I hastened to change the subject, by asking to be shown the famous Blue Chamber, which was said to be haunted. This was the true Mecca of my pilgrimage into Hants.

'It is along this passage,' said Frank, leading the way, 'and not very far from your own quarters. There is nothing in its looks likely to hint at the ghost – at all events by day – but it is haunted for all that.'

Thus speaking he led me into a large room with a low ceiling, and a broad casement looking out onto the untrimmed park, where the woodland was most sylvan. The walls were hung with blue cloth embroidered with grotesque figures in black braid or thread, I know not which. There was a large old-fashioned bed with tester and figured curtains and a quantity of cumbersome furniture of the early Georgian epoch. Not having been inhabited for many years the room had a desolate and silent look – if one may use such an expression – and to my mind looked gruesome enough to conjure up a battalion of ghosts, let alone one.

'I don't agree with you!' said I, in reply to my host's remark. 'To my mind this is the very model of a haunted chamber. What is the legend?'

'I'll tell it to you on Christmas Eve,' replied Ringan, as we left the room. 'It is rather a blood-curdling tale.'

'Do you believe it?' said I, struck by the solemn air of the speaker.

'I have had evidence to make me credulous,' he replied dryly, and closed the subject for the time being.

It was renewed on Christmas Eve when all our company were gathered round a huge wood fire in the library. Outside, the snow lay thick on the ground, and the gaunt trees stood up black and leafless out of the white expanse. The sky was of a frosty blue with sharply twinkling stars, and a hard-looking moon. On the snow the shadows of interlacing boughs were traced blackly as in Indian ink, and the cold was of Arctic severity.

But seated in the holly-decked apartment before a noble fire which roared bravely up the wide chimney we cared nothing for the frozen world out of doors. We laughed and talked, sang songs and recalled adventures, until somewhere about ten o'clock we fell into a ghostly vein quite in keeping with the goblin-haunted season. It was then that Frank Ringan was called upon to chill our blood with his local legend. This he did without much pressing.

'In the reign of the good Queen Anne,' said he, with a gravity befitting the subject, 'my ancestor Hugh Ringan was the owner of this house. He was a silent misanthropic man, having been soured early in life by the treachery of a woman. Mistrusting the sex he refused to marry for many years; and it was not until he was fifty years of age that he was beguiled by the arts of a pretty girl into the toils of matrimony. The lady was Joan Challoner, the daughter of the Earl of Branscourt; and she was esteemed one of the beauties of Queen Anne's court.

'It was in London that Hugh met her, and thinking from her innocent and child-like appearance that she would make him a true-hearted wife, he married her after a six months' courtship and brought her with all honour to Ringshaw Grange. After his marriage he became more cheerful and less distrustful of his fellow creatures. Lady Joan was all to him that a wife could be, and seemed devoted to her husband and child – for she early became a mother – when one Christmas Eve all this happiness came to an end.'

'Oh!' said I, rather cynically. 'So Lady Joan proved to be no better than the rest of her sex.'

'So Hugh Ringan thought, Doctor; but he was as

mistaken as you are. Lady Joan occupied the Blue Room, which I showed you the other day; and on Christmas Eve, when riding home late, Hugh saw a man descend from the window. Thunderstruck by the sight, he galloped after the man and caught him before he could mount a horse which was waiting for him. The cavalier was a handsome young fellow of twenty-five, who refused to answer Hugh's questions. Thinking, naturally enough, that he had to do with a lover of his wife's, Hugh fought a duel with the stranger and killed him after a hard fight.

'Leaving him dead on the snow he rode back to the Grange, and burst in on his wife to accuse her of perfidy. It was in vain that Lady Joan tried to defend herself by stating that the visitor was her brother, who was engaged in plots for the restoration of James II, and on that account wished to keep secret the fact of his presence in England. Hugh did not believe her, and told her plainly that he had killed her lover; whereupon Lady Joan burst out into a volley of reproaches and cursed her husband. Furious at what he deemed was her boldness Hugh at first attempted to kill her, but not thinking the punishment sufficient, he cut off her right hand.'

'Why?' asked everyone, quite unprepared for this information.

'Because in the first place Lady Joan was very proud of her beautiful white hands, and in the second Hugh had seen the stranger kiss her hand – her right hand – before he descended from the window. For these reasons he mutilated her thus terribly.'

'And she died.'

'Yes, a week after her hand was cut off. And she swore

that she would come back to touch all those in the Blue Room – that is who slept in it – who were foredoomed to death. She kept her promise, for many people who have slept in that fatal room have been touched by the dead hand of Lady Joan, and have subsequently died.'

'Did Hugh find out that his wife was innocent?'

'He did,' replied Ringan, 'and within a month after her death. The stranger was really her brother, plotting for James II, as she had stated. Hugh was not punished by man for his crime, but within a year he slept in the Blue Chamber and was found dead next morning with the mark of three fingers on his right wrist. It was thought that in his remorse he had courted death by sleeping in the room cursed by his wife.'

'And there was a mark on him?'

'On his right wrist red marks like a burn; the impression of three fingers. Since that time the room has been haunted.'

'Does everyone who sleeps in it die?' I asked.

'No. Many people have risen well and hearty in the morning. Only those who are doomed to an early death are thus touched!'

'When did the last case occur?'

'Three years ago' was Frank's unexpected reply. 'A friend of mine called Herbert Spencer would sleep in that room. He saw the ghost and was touched. He showed me the marks next morning – three red finger marks.'

'Did the omen hold good?'

'Yes. Spencer died three months afterwards. He was thrown from his horse.'

I was about to put further questions in a sceptical vein, when we heard shouts outside, and we all sprang to our feet as the door was thrown open to admit Miss Laura in a state of excitement.

'Fire! Fire!' she cried, almost distracted. 'Oh! Mr Ringan,' addressing herself to Percy, 'your room is on fire! I—'

We waited to hear no more, but in a body rushed up to Percy's room. Volumes of smoke were rolling out of the door, and flames were flashing within. Frank Ringan, however, was prompt and cool-headed. He had the alarm bell rung, summoned the servants, grooms and stable hands, and in twenty minutes the fire was extinguished.

On asking how the fire had started, Miss Laura, with much hysterical sobbing, stated that she had gone into Percy's room to see that all was ready and comfortable for the night. Unfortunately the wind wafted one of the bed curtains towards the candle she was carrying, and in a moment the room was in a blaze.

After pacifying Miss Laura, who could not help the accident, Frank turned to his cousin. By this time we were back again in the library.

'My dear fellow,' he said, 'your room is swimming in water, and is charred with fire. I'm afraid you can't stay there tonight; but I don't know where to put you unless you take the Blue Room.'

'The Blue Room!' we all cried. 'What! The haunted chamber?'

'Yes; all the other rooms are full. Still, if Percy is afraid—'

'Afraid!' cried Percy indignantly. 'I'm not afraid at all. I'll sleep in the Blue Room with the greatest of pleasure.'

'But the ghost—'

'I don't care for the ghost,' interrupted the Australian,

with a nervous laugh. 'We have no ghosts in our part of the world, and as I have not seen one, I do not believe there is such a thing.'

We all tried to dissuade him from sleeping in the haunted room, and several of us offered to give up our apartments for the night – Frank among the number. But Percy's dignity was touched, and he was resolute to keep his word. He had plenty of pluck, as I said before, and the fancy that we might think him a coward spurred him on to resist our entreaties.

The end of it was that shortly before midnight he went off to the Blue Room, and declared his intention of sleeping in it. There was nothing more to be said in the face of such obstinacy, so one by one we retired, quite unaware of the events to happen before the morning, So on that Christmas Eve the Blue Room had an unexpected tenant.

On going to my bedroom I could not sleep. The tale told by Frank Ringan haunted my fancy, and the idea of Percy sleeping in that ill-omened room made me nervous. I did not believe in ghosts myself, nor, so far as I knew, did Percy, but the little man suffered from heart disease – he was strung up to a high nervous pitch by our ghost stories – and if anything out of the common – even from natural causes – happened in that room, the shock might be fatal to its occupant.

I knew well enough that Percy, out of pride, would refuse to give up the room, yet I was determined that he should not sleep in it; so, failing persuasion, I employed stratagem. I had my medicine chest with me, and taking it from my portmanteau I prepared a powerful narcotic. I left this on the table and went along to the Blue Room, which, as I have said before, was not very far from mine.

A knock brought Percy to the door, clothed in pyjamas, and at a glance I could see that the ghostly atmosphere of the place was already telling on his nerves. He looked pale and disturbed, but his mouth was firmly set with an obstinate expression likely to resist my proposals. However, out of diplomacy, I made none, but blandly stated my errand, with more roughness, indeed, than was necessary.

'Come to my room, Percy,' I said, when he appeared, 'and let me give you something to calm your nerves.'

'I'm not afraid!' he said, defiantly.

'Who said you were?' I rejoined, tartly. 'You believe in ghosts no more than I do, so why should you be afraid? But after the alarm of fire your nerves are upset, and I want to give you something to put them right. Otherwise, you'll get no sleep.'

'I shouldn't mind a composing draught, certainly,' said the little man. 'Have you it here?'

'No, it's in my room, a few yards off. Come along.'

Quite deluded by my speech and manner, Percy followed me into my bedroom, and obediently enough swallowed the medicine. Then I made him sit down in a comfortable arm-chair, on the plea that he must not walk immediately after the draught. The result of my experiment was justified, for in less than ten minutes the poor little man was fast asleep under the influence of the narcotic. When thus helpless, I placed him on my bed, quite satisfied that he would not awaken until late the next day. My task accomplished, I extinguished the light, and went off myself to the Blue Room, intending to remain there for the night.

It may be asked why I did so, as I could easily have taken

my rest on the sofa in my own room; but the fact is, I was anxious to sleep in a haunted chamber. I did not believe in ghosts, as I had never seen one, but as there was a chance of meeting here with an authentic phantom I did not wish to lose the opportunity.

Therefore when I saw that Percy was safe for the night, I took up my quarters in the ghostly territory, with much curiosity, but — as I can safely aver — no fear. All the same, in case of practical jokes on the part of the feather-headed young men in the house, I took my revolver with me. Thus prepared, I locked the door of the Blue Room and slipped into bed, leaving the light burning. The revolver I kept under my pillow ready to my hand in case of necessity.

'Now,' said I grimly, as I made myself comfortable, 'I'm ready for ghosts, or goblins, or practical jokers.'

I lay awake for a long time, staring at the queer figures on the blue draperies of the apartment. In the pale flame of the candle they looked ghostly enough to disturb the nerves of anyone: and when the draught fluttered the tapestries the figures seemed to move as though alive. For this sight alone I was glad that Percy had not slept in that room. I could fancy the poor man lying in that vast bed with blanched face and beating heart, listening to every creak, and watching the fantastic embroideries waving on the walls. Brave as he was, I am sure the sounds and sights of that room would have shaken his nerves. I did not feel very comfortable myself, sceptic as I was.

When the candle had burned down pretty low I fell asleep. How long I slumbered I know not: but I woke up with the impression that something or someone was in the room. The candle had wasted nearly to the socket and the flame was flickering and leaping fitfully, so as to display the room one moment and leave it almost in darkness the next. I heard a soft step crossing the room, and as it drew near a sudden spurt of flame from the candle showed me a little woman standing by the side of the bed. She was dressed in a gown of flowered brocade, and wore the towering head dress of the Queen Anne epoch. Her face I could scarcely see, as the flash of flame was only momentary: but I felt what the Scotch call a deadly grue as I realised that this was the veritable phantom of Lady Joan.

For the moment the natural dread of the supernatural quite overpowered me, and with my hands and arms lying outside the counterpane I rested inert and chilled with fear. This sensation of helplessness in the presence of evil was like what one experiences in a nightmare of the worst kind.

When again the flame of the expiring candle shot up, I beheld the ghost close at hand, and – as I felt rather than saw – knew that it was bending over me. A faint odour of musk was in the air, and I heard the soft rustle of the brocaded skirts echo through the semi-darkness. The next moment I felt my right wrist gripped in a burning grasp, and the sudden pain roused my nerves from their paralysis.

With a yell I rolled over, away from the ghost, wrenching my wrist from that horrible clasp, and, almost mad with pain I groped with my left hand for the revolver. As I seized it the candle flared up for the last time, and I saw the ghost gliding back towards the tapestries. In a second I raised the revolver and fired. The next moment there was a wild cry of terror and agony, the fall of a heavy body on the floor, and almost before I knew where I was I found myself outside the door of the haunted room. To attract attention I fired another shot from my revolver, while the Thing on the floor moaned in the darkness most horribly.

In a few moments guests and servants, all in various stages of undress, came rushing along the passage bearing lights. A babel of voices arose, and I managed to babble some incoherent explanation, and led the way into the room. There on the floor lay the ghost, and we lowered the candles to look at its face. I sprang up with a cry on recognising who it was.

'Frank Ringan!'

It was indeed Frank Ringan disguised as a woman in wig and brocades. He looked at me with a ghostly face, his mouth working nervously. With an effort he raised himself on his hands and tried to speak – whether in confession or exculpation, I know not. But the attempt was too much for him, a choking cry escaped his lips, a jet of blood burst from his mouth, and he fell back dead.

Over the rest of the events of that terrible night I draw a veil. There are some things it is as well not to speak of. Only I may state that all through the horror and confusion Percy Ringan, thanks to my strong sleeping draught, slumbered as peacefully as a child, thereby saving his life.

With the morning's light came discoveries and explanations. We found one of the panels behind the tapestry of the Blue Room open, and it gave admittance into a passage which on examination proved to lead into Frank Ringan's bedroom. On the floor we discovered a delicate hand formed of steel, and which bore marks of having been in the fire. On my right wrist were three distinct burns, which I have no hesitation in declaring were caused by the mechanical hand which we picked up near the dead man. And the explanation of these things came from Miss Laura, who was wild with terror at the death of her master, and said in her first outburst of grief and fear, what I am sure she regretted in her calmer moments.

'It's all Frank's fault,' she wept. 'He was poor and wished to be rich. He got Percy to make his will in his favour, and wanted to kill him by a shock. He knew that Percy had heart disease and that a shock might prove fatal; so he contrived that his cousin should sleep in the Blue Room on Christmas Eve; and he himself played the ghost of Lady Joan with the burning hand. It was a steel hand, which he heated in his own room so as to mark with a scar those it touched.'

'Whose idea was this?' I asked, horrified by the devilish ingenuity of the scheme.

'Frank's!' said Miss Laura, candidly. 'He promised to marry me if I helped him to get the money by Percy's death. We found that there was a secret passage leading to the Blue Room; so some years ago we invented the story that it was haunted.'

'Why, in God's name?'

'Because Frank was always poor. He knew that his cousin in Australia had heart disease, and invited him home to kill him with fright. To make things safe he was always talking about the haunted room and telling the story so that everything should be ready for Percy on his arrival. Our plans were all carried out. Percy arrived and Frank got him to make the will in his favour. Then he was told the story of Lady Joan and her hand, and by setting fire to Percy's room last night I got him to sleep in the Blue Chamber without any suspicion being aroused.'

'You wicked woman!' I cried. 'Did you fire Percy's room on purpose?'

'Yes. Frank promised to marry me if I helped him. We had to get Percy to sleep in the Blue Chamber, and I managed it by setting fire to his bedroom. He would have died with fright when Frank, as Lady Joan, touched him with the steel hand, and no one would have been the wiser. Your sleeping in that haunted room saved Percy's life, Dr Lascelles, yet Frank invited you down as part of his scheme, that you might examine the body and declare the death to be a natural one.'

'Was it Frank who burnt the wrist of Herbert Spencer some years ago?' I asked.

'Yes!' replied Miss Laura, wiping her red eyes. 'We thought if the ghost appeared to a few other people, that Percy's death might seem more natural. It was a mere coincidence that Mr Spencer died three months after the ghost touched him.'

'Do you know you are a very wicked woman, Miss Laura?'

'I am a very unhappy one,' she retorted. 'I have lost the only man I ever loved; and his miserable cousin survives to step into his shoes as the master of Ringshaw Grange.'

That was the sole conversation I had with the wretched woman, for shortly afterwards she disappeared, and I fancy must have gone abroad, as she was never more heard of. At the inquest held on the body of Frank the whole strange story came out, and was reported at full length by the London press to the dismay of ghost-seers: for the fame of Ringshaw Grange as a haunted mansion had been great in the land.

I was afraid lest the jury should bring in a verdict of manslaughter against me, but the peculiar features of the case being taken into consideration I was acquitted of blame, and shortly afterwards returned to India with an unblemished character. Percy Ringan was terribly distressed on hearing of his cousin's death, and shocked by the discovery of his treachery. However, he was consoled by becoming the head of the family, and as he lives a quiet life at Ringshaw Grange there is not much chance of his early death from heart disease – at all events from a ghostly point of view.

The Blue Chamber is shut up, for it is haunted now by a worse spectre than that of Lady Joan, whose legend (purely fictitious) was so ingeniously set forth by Frank. It is haunted by the ghost of the cold-blooded scoundrel who fell into his own trap; and who met with his death in the very moment he was contriving that of another man. As to myself, I have given up ghost-hunting and sleeping in haunted rooms. Nothing will ever tempt me to experiment in that way again. One adventure of that sort is enough to last me a lifetime.

An Unlocked Window

Ethel Lina White

'Have you locked up, Nurse Cherry?'

'Yes, Nurse Silver.'

'Every door? Every window?'

'Yes, yes.'

Yet even as she shot home the last bolt of the front door, at the back of Nurse Cherry's mind was a vague misgiving.

She had forgotten – *something*.

She was young and pretty, but her expression was anxious. While she had most of the qualities to ensure professional success, she was always on guard against a serious handicap.

She had a bad memory.

Hitherto, it had betrayed her only in burnt Benger and an occasional overflow in the bathroom. But yesterday's lapse was little short of a calamity.

Late that afternoon she had discovered the oxygen

cylinder, which she had been last to use, empty – its cap care-lessly unscrewed.

The disaster called for immediate remedy, for the patient, Professor Glendower Baker, was suffering from the effects of gas poisoning. Although dark was falling, the man, Iles, had to harness the pony for the long drive over the mountains, in order to get a fresh supply.

Nurse Cherry had sped his parting with a feeling of loss. Iles was a cheery soul and a tower of strength.

It was dirty weather with a spitting rain blanketing the elephant-grey mounds of the surrounding hills. The valley road wound like a muddy coil between soaked bracken and dwarf oaks.

Iles shook his head as he regarded the savage isolation of the landscape.

'I don't half like leaving you – a pack of women – with *him* about. Put up the shutters on every door and window, Nurse, and don't let *no one* come in till I get back.'

He drove off – his lamps glow-worms in the gloom.

Darkness and rain. And the sodden undergrowth seemed to quiver and blur, so that stunted trees took on the shapes of crouching men advancing towards the house.

Nurse Cherry hurried through her round of fastening the windows. As she carried her candle from room to room of the upper floors, she had the uneasy feeling that she was visible to any watcher.

Her mind kept wandering back to the bad business of the forgotten cylinder. It had plunged her in depths of self-distrust and shame. She was overtired, having nursed the patient single-handed, until the arrival, three days ago, of the second nurse. But that fact did not absolve her from blame.

'I'm not fit to be a nurse,' she told herself in bitter self-reproach.

She was still in a dream when she locked the front door. Nurse Silver's questions brought her back to earth with a furtive sense of guilt.

Nurse Silver's appearance inspired confidence, for she was of solid build, with strong features and a black shingle. Yet, for all her stout looks, her nature seemed that of Job.

'Has he gone?' she asked in her harsh voice.

'Iles? Yes.'

Nurse Cherry repeated his caution.

'He'll get back as soon as he can,' she added, 'but it probably won't be until dawn.'

'Then,' said Nurse Silver gloomily, 'we are *alone*.'

Nurse Cherry laughed.

'Alone? Three hefty women, all of us able to give a good account of ourselves.'

'*I'm* not afraid.' Nurse Silver gave her rather a peculiar look. '*I'm* safe enough.'

'Why?'

'Because of *you*. He won't touch me with you here.'

Nurse Cherry tried to belittle her own attractive appearance with a laugh.

'For that matter,' she said, 'we are all safe.'

'Do you think so? A lonely house. No man. And two of *us*.'

Nurse Cherry glanced at her starched nurse's apron. Nurse Silver's words made her feel like special bait — a goat tethered in a jungle, to attract a tiger.

'Don't talk nonsense,' she said sharply.

The countryside, of late, had been chilled by a series of murders. In each case, the victim had been a trained nurse. The police were searching for a medical student – Sylvester Leek. It was supposed that his mind had become unhinged, consequent on being jilted by a pretty probationer. He had disappeared from the hospital after a violent breakdown during an operation.

Next morning, a night nurse had been discovered in the laundry – strangled. Four days later, a second nurse had been horribly done to death in the garden of a villa on the outskirts of the small agricultural town. After the lapse of a fortnight, one of the nurses in attendance on Sir Thomas Jones had been discovered in her bedroom – throttled.

The last murder had taken place in a large mansion in the very heart of the country. Every isolated cottage and farm became infected with panic. Women barred their doors and no girl lingered late in the lane, without her lover.

Nurse Cherry wished she could forget the details she had read in the newspapers. The ingenuity with which the poor victims had been lured to their doom and the ferocity of the attacks all proved a diseased brain driven by malignant motive.

It was a disquieting thought that she and Nurse Silver were localised. Professor Baker had succumbed to gas poisoning while engaged in work of national importance and his illness had been reported in the press.

'In any case,' she argued, 'how could – *he* – know that we're left tonight?'

Nurse Silver shook her head.

'*They* always know.'

'Rubbish! And he's probably committed suicide by now. There hasn't been a murder for over a month.'

'Exactly. There's bound to be another, *soon*.'

Nurse Cherry thought of the undergrowth creeping nearer to the house. Her nerve snapped.

'Are you trying to make me afraid?'

'Yes,' said Nurse Silver, 'I am. I don't trust you. You forget.'

Nurse Cherry coloured angrily.

'You might let me forget that wretched cylinder.'

'But you might forget again.'

'Not likely.'

As she uttered the words — like oil spreading over water — her mind was smeared with doubt.

Something forgotten.

She shivered as she looked up the well of the circular staircase, which was dimly lit by an oil lamp suspended to a crossbar. Shadows rode the walls and wiped out the ceiling like a flock of sooty bats.

An eerie place. Hiding holes on every landing.

The house was tall and narrow, with two or three rooms on every floor. It was rather like a tower or a pepper pot. The semi-basement was occupied by the kitchen and domestic offices. On the ground floor were a sitting room, the dining room and the professor's study. The first floor was devoted to the patient. On the second floor were the bedrooms of the nurses and of the Iles couple. The upper floors were given up to the professor's laboratorial work.

Nurse Cherry remembered the stout shutters and the

secure hasps. There had been satisfaction in turning the house into a fortress. But now, instead of a sense of security, she had a feeling of being caged.

She moved to the staircase.

'While we're bickering,' she said, 'we're neglecting the patient.'

Nurse Silver called her back.

'I'm on duty now.'

Professional etiquette forbade any protest. But Nurse Cherry looked after her colleague with sharp envy.

She thought of the professor's fine brow, his wasted clear-cut features and visionary slate-grey eyes, with yearning. For after three years of nursing children, with an occasional mother or aunt, romance had entered her life.

From the first, she had been interested in her patient. She had scarcely eaten or slept until the crisis had passed. She noticed too, how his eyes followed her around the room and how he could hardly bear her out of his sight.

Yesterday he had held her hand in his thin fingers.

'Marry me, Stella,' he whispered.

'Not unless you get well,' she answered foolishly.

Since then, he had called her 'Stella'. Her name was music in her ears until her rapture was dashed by the fatal episode of the cylinder. She had to face the knowledge that, in case of another relapse, Glendower's life hung upon a thread.

She was too wise to think further, so she began to speculate on Nurse Silver's character. Hitherto, they had met only at meals, when she had been taciturn and moody.

Tonight she had revealed a personal animus against herself, and Nurse Cherry believed she guessed its cause.

The situation was a hotbed for jealousy. Two women were thrown into close contact with a patient and a doctor, both of whom were bachelors. Although Nurse Silver was the ill-favoured one, it was plain that she possessed her share of personal vanity. Nurse Cherry noticed, from her painful walk, that she wore shoes which were too small. More than that, she had caught her in the act of scrutinising her face in the mirror.

These rather pitiful glimpses into the dark heart of the warped woman made Nurse Cherry uneasy.

The house was very still; she missed Nature's sounds of rain or wind against the windowpane and the cheerful voices of the Iles couple. The silence might be a background for sounds she did not wish to hear.

She spoke aloud, for the sake of hearing her own voice.

'Cheery if Silver plays up tonight. Well, well! I'll hurry up Mrs Iles with the supper.'

Her spirits rose as she opened the door leading to the basement. The warm spicy odour of the kitchen floated up the short staircase and she could see a bar of yellow light from the half-opened door.

When she entered, she saw no sign of supper. Mrs Iles – a strapping blonde with strawberry cheeks – sat at the kitchen table, her head buried in her huge arms.

As Nurse Cherry shook her gently, she raised her head.

'Eh?' she said stupidly.

'Gracious, Mrs Iles. Are you ill?'

'Eh? Feel as if I'd one over the eight.'

'What on earth d'you mean?'

'What *you* call "tight". Love-a-duck, my head's that swimmy—'

Nurse Cherry looked suspiciously at an empty glass upon the dresser, as Mrs Iles's head dropped like a bleached sunflower.

Nurse Silver heard her hurrying footsteps on the stairs. She met her upon the landing.

'Anything wrong?'

'Mrs Iles. I think she's drunk. Do come and see.'

When Nurse Silver reached the kitchen, she hoisted Mrs Iles under the armpits and set her on unsteady feet.

'Obvious,' she said. 'Help get her upstairs.'

It was no easy task to drag twelve stone of protesting Mrs Iles up three flights of stairs.

'She feels like a centipede, with every pair of feet going in a different direction,' Nurse Cherry panted, as they reached the door of the Ileses' bedroom. 'I can manage her now, thank you.'

She wished Nurse Silver would go back to the patient, instead of looking at her with that fixed expression.

'What are you staring at?' she asked sharply.

'Has nothing struck you as *strange*?'

'What?'

In the dim light, Nurse Silver's eyes looked like empty black pits.

'Today,' she said, 'there were four of us. First, Iles goes. Now, Mrs Iles. That leaves only two. If anything happens to you or me, there'll only be *one*.'

As Nurse Cherry put Mrs Iles to bed, she reflected that Nurse Silver was decidedly not a cheerful companion. She made a natural sequence of events appear in the light of a sinister conspiracy.

Nurse Cherry reminded herself sharply that Iles's absence was due to her own carelessness, while his wife was addicted to her glass.

Still, some unpleasant suggestion remained, like the sediment from a splash of muddy water. She found herself thinking with horror of some calamity befalling Nurse Silver. If she were left by herself she felt she would lose her senses with fright.

It was an unpleasant picture. The empty house — a dark shell for lurking shadows. No one on whom to depend. Her patient — a beloved burden and responsibility.

It was better not to think of that. But she kept on thinking. The outside darkness seemed to be pressing against the walls, bending them in. As her fears multiplied, the medical student changed from a human being with a distraught brain, to a Force, cunning and insatiable — a ravening blood-monster.

Nurse Silver's words recurred to her.

'*They* always know.' Even so. Doors might be locked, but *they* would find a way inside.

Her nerves tingled at the sound of the telephone bell, ringing far below in the hall.

She kept looking over her shoulder as she ran downstairs. She took off the receiver in positive panic, lest she should be greeted with a maniac scream of laughter.

It was a great relief to hear the homely Welsh accent of Dr Jones.

He had serious news for her. As she listened, her heart began to thump violently.

'Thank you, Doctor, for letting me know,' she said. 'Please ring up directly you hear more.'

'Hear more of what?'

Nurse Cherry started at Nurse Silver's harsh voice. She had come downstairs noiselessly in her soft nursing slippers.

'It's only the doctor,' she said, trying to speak lightly. 'He's thinking of changing the medicine.'

'Then why are you so white? You are shaking.'

Nurse Cherry decided that the truth would serve her best.

'To be honest,' she said, 'I've just had bad news. Something ghastly. I didn't want you to know, for there's no sense in two of us being frightened. But now I come to think of it, you ought to feel reassured.'

She forced a smile.

'You said there'd have to be another murder soon. Well — there *has* been one.'

'Where? Who? Quick.'

Nurse Cherry understood what is meant by the infection of fear as Nurse Silver gripped her arm.

In spite of her effort at self-mastery, there was a quiver in her own voice.

'It's a — a hospital nurse. Strangled. They've just found the body in a quarry and they sent for Dr Jones to make the examination. The police are trying to establish her identity.'

Nurse Silver's eyes were wide and staring.

'Another hospital nurse? That makes *four*.'

She turned on the younger woman in sudden suspicion.

'Why did he ring you up?'

Nurse Cherry did not want that question.

'To tell us to be specially on guard,' she replied.

'You mean — he's near?'

'Of course not. The doctor said the woman had been dead three or four days. By now, he'll be far away.'

'Or he may be even nearer than you think.'

Nurse Cherry glanced involuntarily at the barred front door. Her head felt as if it were bursting. It was impossible to think connectedly. But – somewhere – beating its wings like a caged bird, was the incessant reminder.

Something forgotten.

The sight of the elder woman's twitching lips reminded her that she had to be calm for two.

'Go back to the patient,' she said, 'while I get the supper. We'll both feel better after something to eat.'

In spite of her new-born courage, it needed an effort of will to descend into the basement. So many doors, leading to scullery, larder and coal cellar, all smelling of mice. So many hiding places.

The kitchen proved a cheerful antidote to depression. The caked fire in the open range threw a red glow upon the Welsh dresser and the canisters labelled 'Sugar' and 'Tea'. A sandy cat slept upon the rag mat. Everything looked safe and homely.

Quickly collecting bread, cheese, a round of beef, a cold white shape, and stewed prunes, she piled them on a tray. She added stout for Nurse Silver and made cocoa for herself. As she watched the milk froth up through the dark mixture and inhaled the steaming odour, she felt that her fears were baseless and absurd.

She sang as she carried her tray upstairs. She was going to marry Glendower.

The nurses used the bedroom which connected with the

sick chamber for their meals, in order to be near the patient. As the night nurse entered, Nurse Cherry strained her ears for the sound of Glendower's voice. She longed for one glimpse of him. Even a smile would help.

'How's the patient?' she asked.

'All right.'

'Could I have a peep?'

'No. You're off duty.'

As the women sat down, Nurse Cherry was amused to notice that Nurse Silver kicked off her tight shoes.

'You seem very interested in the patient, Nurse Cherry,' she remarked sourly.

'I have a right to feel rather interested.' Nurse Cherry smiled as she cut bread. 'The doctor gives me the credit for his being alive.'

'Ah! But the doctor thinks the world of you.'

Nurse Cherry was not conceited, but she was human enough to know that she had made a conquest of the big Welshman.

The green glow of jealousy in Nurse Silver's eyes made her reply guardedly.

'Dr Jones is decent to everyone.'

But she was of too friendly and impulsive a nature to keep her secret bottled up. She reminded herself that they were two women sharing an ordeal and she tried to establish some link of friendship.

'I feel you despise me,' she said. 'You think me lacking in self-control. And you can't forget that cylinder. But really, I've gone through such an awful strain. For four nights, I never took off my clothes.'

'Why didn't you have a second nurse?'

'There was the expense. The professor gives his whole life to enrich the nation and he's poor. Then, later, I felt I *must* do everything for him myself. I didn't want you, only Dr Jones said I was heading for a breakdown.'

She looked at her left hand, seeing there the shadowy outline of a wedding ring.

'Don't think me sloppy, but I must tell someone. The professor and I are going to get married.'

'*If* he lives.'

'But he's turned the corner now.'

'Don't count your chickens.'

Nurse Cherry felt a stab of fear.

'Are you hiding something from me? Is he – worse?'

'No. He's the same. I was thinking that Dr Jones might interfere. You've led him on, haven't you? I've seen you smile at him. It's light women like you that make the trouble in the world.'

Nurse Cherry was staggered by the injustice of the attack. But as she looked at the elder woman's working face, she saw that she was consumed by jealousy. One life lay in the shadow, the other in the sun. The contrast was too sharp.

'We won't quarrel tonight,' she said gently. 'We're going through rather a bad time together and we have only each other to depend on. I'm just clinging to *you*. If anything were to happen to you, like Mrs Iles, I should jump out of my skin with fright.'

Nurse Silver was silent for a minute.

'I never thought of that,' she said presently. 'Only us two. And all these empty rooms, above and below. What's that?'

From the hall, came the sound of muffled knocking.

Nurse Cherry sprang to her feet.

'Someone's at the front door.'

Nurse Silver's fingers closed round her arm, like iron hoops.

'Sit down. It's *him*.'

The two women stared at each other as the knocking continued. It was loud and insistent. To Nurse Cherry's ears, it carried a message of urgency.

'I'm going down,' she said. 'It may be Dr Jones.'

'How could you tell?'

'By his voice.'

'You fool. Anyone could imitate *his* accent.'

Nurse Cherry saw the beads break out round Nurse Silver's mouth. Her fear had the effect of steadying her own nerves.

'I'm going down, to find out who it is,' she said. 'It may be important news about the murder.'

Nurse Silver dragged her away from the door.

'What did I say? *You* are the danger. You've forgotten already.'

'Forgotten – what?'

'Didn't Iles tell you to open to no one? *No one?*'

Nurse Cherry hung her head. She sat down in shamed silence.

The knocking ceased. Presently they heard it again at the back door.

Nurse Silver wiped her face.

'He *means* to get in.' She laid her hand on Nurse Cherry's arm. 'You're not even trembling. Are you never afraid?'

'Only of ghosts.'

In spite of her brave front, Nurse Cherry was inwardly quaking at her own desperate resolution. Nurse Silver had justly accused her of endangering the household. Therefore it was her plain duty to make once more the round of the house, either to see what she had forgotten, or to lay the doubt.

'I'm going upstairs,' she said. 'I want to look out.'

'Unbar a window?' Nurse Silver's agitation rose in a gale. 'You shall *not*. It's murdering folly. Think! That last nurse was found dead *inside* her bedroom.'

'All right. I won't.'

'You'd best be careful. You've been trying to spare me, but perhaps I've been trying to spare you. I'll only say this. *There is something strange happening in this house.*'

Nurse Cherry felt a chill at her heart. Only, since she was a nurse, she knew that it was really the pit of her stomach. Something wrong? If through her wretched memory, she again were the culprit, she must expiate her crime by shielding the others, at any risk to herself.

She had to force herself to mount the stairs. Her candle, flickering in the draught, peopled the walls with distorted shapes. When she reached the top landing, without stopping to think, she walked resolutely into the laboratory and the adjoining room.

Both were securely barred and empty. Gaining courage, she entered the attic. Under its window was a precipitous slope of roof without gutter or waterpipe, to give finger-hold. Knowing that it would be impossible for anyone to gain an entry, she opened the shutter and unfastened the window.

The cold air on her face refreshed her and restored her to

calm. She realised that she had been suffering to a certain extent from claustrophobia.

The rain had ceased and a wind arisen. She could see a young harried moon flying through the clouds. The dark humps of the hills were visible against the darkness, but nothing more.

She remained at the window for some time, thinking of Glendower. It was a solace to remember the happiness which awaited her once this night of terror was over.

Presently the urge to see him grew too strong to be resisted. Nurse Silver's words had made her uneasy on his behalf. Even though she offended the laws of professional etiquette, she determined to see for herself that all was well.

Leaving the window open so that some air might percolate into the house, she slipped stealthily downstairs. She stopped on the second floor to visit her own room and that of Nurse Silver. All was quiet and secure. In her own quarters, Mrs Iles still snored in the sleep of the unjust.

There were two doors to the patient's room. The one led to the nurses' room where Nurse Silver was still at her meal. The other led to the landing.

Directly Nurse Cherry entered, she knew that her fear had been the premonition of love. Something was seriously amiss. Glendower's head tossed uneasily on the pillow. His face was deeply flushed. When she called him by name, he stared at her, his luminous grey eyes ablaze.

He did not recognise her, for instead of 'Stella', he called her 'Nurse'.

'Nurse, Nurse.' He mumbled something that sounded like 'man' and then slipped back in her arms, unconscious.

Nurse Silver entered the room at her cry. As she felt his pulse, she spoke with dry significance.

'We could do with oxygen now.'

Nurse Cherry could only look at her with piteous eyes.

'Shall I telephone for Dr Jones?' she asked humbly.

'Yes.'

It seemed like the continuation of an evil dream when she could get no answer to her ring. Again and again she tried desperately to galvanise the dead instrument.

Presently Nurse Silver appeared on the landing.

'Is the doctor coming?'

'I – I can't get any answer.' Nurse Cherry forced back her tears. 'Oh, whatever can be wrong?'

'Probably a wet creeper twisted round the wire. But it doesn't matter now. The patient is sleeping.'

Nurse Cherry's face registered no comfort. As though the shocks of the last few minutes had set in motion the arrested machinery of her brain, she remembered suddenly what she had forgotten.

The larder window.

She recollected now what had happened. When she entered the larder on her round of locking up, a mouse had run over her feet. She ran to fetch the cat which chased it into a hole in the kitchen. In the excitement of the incident, she had forgotten to return to close the window.

Her heart leapt violently at the realisation that, all these hours, the house had been open to any marauder. Even while she and Nurse Silver had listened, shivering, to the knocking at the door, she had already betrayed the fortress.

'What's the matter?' asked Nurse Silver.

'Nothing. Nothing.'

She dared not tell the older woman. Even now it was not too late to remedy her omission.

In her haste she no longer feared the descent into the basement. She could hardly get down the stairs with sufficient speed. As she entered the larder the wire-covered window flapped in the breeze. She secured it and was just entering the kitchen, when her eye fell on a dark patch on the passage.

It was the footprint of a man.

Nurse Cherry remembered that Iles had been in the act of getting fresh coal into the cellar when he had been called away to make his journey. He had no time to clean up and the floor was still sooty with rain-soaked dust.

As she raised her candle, the footprint gleamed faintly. Stooping hastily, she touched it.

It was still damp.

At first she stood as if petrified, staring at it stupidly. Then as she realised that in front of her lay a freshly made imprint, her nerve snapped completely. With a scream, she dropped her candle and tore up the stairs, calling on Nurse Silver.

She was answered by a strange voice. It was thick, heavy, indistinct. A voice she had never heard before.

Knowing not what awaited her on the other side of the door, yet driven on by the courage of ultimate fear, she rushed into the nurses' sitting room.

No one was there save Nurse Silver. She sagged back in her chair, her eyes half-closed, her mouth open.

From her lips issued a second uncouth cry.

Nurse Cherry put her arm around her.

'What is it? Try to tell me.'

It was plain that Nurse Silver was trying to warn her of some peril. She pointed to her glass and fought for articulation.

'Drugs. Listen. When you lock out, you lock *in*.' Even as she spoke her eyes turned up horribly, exposing the balls in a blind white stare.

Almost mad with terror, Nurse Cherry tried to revive her. Mysteriously, through some unknown agency, what she had dreaded had come to pass.

She was alone.

And somewhere — within the walls of the house — lurked a being, cruel and cunning, who — one after another — had removed each obstacle between himself and his objective.

He had marked down his victim. *Herself.*

In that moment she went clean over the edge of fear. She felt that it was not herself — Stella Cherry — but a stranger in the blue print uniform of a hospital nurse, who calmly speculated on her course of action.

It was impossible to lock herself in the patient's room, for the key was stiff from disuse. And she had not the strength to move furniture which was sufficiently heavy to barricade the door.

The idea of flight was immediately dismissed. In order to get help, she would have to run miles. She could not leave Glendower and two helpless women at the mercy of the baffled maniac.

There was nothing to be done. Her place was by Glendower. She sat down by his bed and took his hand in hers.

The time seemed endless. Her watch seemed sometimes to leap whole hours and then to crawl, as she waited — listening to the myriad sounds in a house at nightfall. There were faint rustlings, the cracking of woodwork, the scamper of mice.

And a hundred times, someone seemed to steal up the stairs and linger just outside her door.

It was nearly three o'clock when suddenly a gong began to beat inside her temples. In the adjoining room was the unmistakable tramp of a man's footsteps.

It was no imagination on her part. They circled the room and then advanced deliberately towards the connecting door.

She saw the handle begin to turn slowly.

In one bound, she reached the door and rushed onto the landing and up the stairs. For a second, she paused before her own room. But its windows were barred and its door had no key. She could not be done to death there in the dark.

As she paused, she heard the footsteps on the stairs. They advanced slowly, driving her on before them. Demented with terror, she fled up to the top storey, instinctively seeking the open window.

She could go no higher. At the attic door, she waited.

Something black appeared on the staircase wall. It was the shadow of her pursuer – a grotesque and distorted herald of crime.

Nurse Cherry gripped the balustrade to keep herself from falling. Everything was growing dark. She knew that she was on the point of fainting, when she was revived by sheer astonishment and joy.

Above the balustrade appeared the head of Nurse Silver.

Nurse Cherry called out to her in warning.

'Come quickly. There's a man in the house.'

She saw Nurse Silver start and fling back her head, as

though in alarm. Then occurred the culminating horror of a night of dread.

A mouse ran across the passage. Raising her heavy shoe, Nurse Silver stamped upon it, grinding her heel upon the tiny creature's head.

In that moment, Nurse Cherry knew the truth. Nurse Silver was a man.

Her brain raced with lightning velocity. It was like a searchlight, piercing the shadows and making the mystery clear.

She knew that the real Nurse Silver had been murdered by Sylvester Leek, on her way to the case. It was her strangled body which had just been found in the quarry. And the murderer had taken her place. The police description was that of a slightly-built youth, with refined features. It would be easy for him to assume the disguise of a woman. He had the necessary medical knowledge to pose as nurse. Moreover, as he had the night shift, no one in the house had come into close contact with him, save the patient.

But the patient had guessed the truth.

To silence his tongue, the killer had drugged him, even as he had disposed of the obstructing presence of Mrs Iles. It was he, too, who had emptied the oxygen cylinder, to get Iles out of the way.

Yet, although he had been alone with his prey for hours, he had held his hand.

Nurse Cherry, with her new mental lucidity, knew the reason. There is a fable that the serpent slavers its victim before swallowing it. In like manner, the maniac – before her final destruction – had wished to coat her with the foul saliva of fear.

All the evening he had been trying to terrorise her — plucking at each jangled nerve up to the climax of his feigned unconsciousness.

Yet she knew that he in turn was fearful lest he should be frustrated in the commission of his crime. Since his victim's body had been discovered in the quarry, the establishment of her identity would mark his hiding place. While Nurse Cherry was at the attic window, he had cut the telephone wire and donned his own shoes for purposes of flight.

She remembered his emotion during the knocking at the door. It was probable that it was Dr Jones who stood without, come to assure himself that she was not alarmed. Had it been the police, they would have effected an entry. The incident proved that nothing had been discovered and that it was useless to count on outside help.

She had to face it — alone.

In the dim light from the young moon, she saw the murderer enter the attic. The grotesque travesty of his nursing disguise added to the terror of the moment.

His eyes were fixed on the open window. It was plain that he was pretending to connect it with the supposed intruder. She in her turn had unconsciously deceived him. He probably knew nothing of the revealing footprint he had left in the basement passage.

'Shut the window, you damned fool,' he shouted.

As he leaned over the low ledge to reach the swinging casement window, Nurse Cherry rushed at him in the instinctive madness of self-defence — thrusting him forward, over the sill.

She had one glimpse of dark distorted features blotting

out the moon and of arms sawing the air, like a starfish, in a desperate attempt to balance.

The next moment, nothing was there.

She sank to the ground, covering her ears with her hands to deaden the sound of the sickening slide over the tiled roof.

It was a long time before she was able to creep down to her patient's room. Directly she entered, its peace healed her like balm. Glendower slept quietly — a half-smile playing round his lips as though he dreamed of her.

Thankfully she went from room to room, unbarring each window and unlocking each door — letting in the dawn.

The Mystery of the
Sleeping-Car Express

Freeman Wills Crofts

No one who was in England in the autumn of 1909 can fail to remember the terrible tragedy which took place in a North-Western express between Preston and Carlisle. The affair attracted enormous attention at the time, not only because of the arresting nature of the events themselves, but even more for the absolute mystery in which they were shrouded.

Quite lately a singular chance has revealed to me the true explanation of the terrible drama, and it is at the express desire of its chief actor that I now take upon myself to make the facts known. As it is a long time since 1909, I may, perhaps, be pardoned if I first recall the events which came to light at the time.

One Thursday, then, early in November of the year in question, the 10.30 p.m. sleeping-car train left Euston as usual for Edinburgh, Glasgow and the North. It was generally a heavy train, being popular with businessmen who liked to complete their day's work in London, sleep while travelling, and arrive at their northern destination with time for a leisurely bath and breakfast before office hours. The night in question was no exception to the rule, and two engines hauled behind them eight large sleeping-cars, two firsts, two thirds and two vans, half of which went to Glasgow, and the remainder to Edinburgh.

It is essential to the understanding of what follows that the composition of the rear portion of the train should be remembered. At the extreme end came the Glasgow van, a long eight-wheeled, bogie vehicle, with Guard Jones in charge. Next to the van was one of the third-class coaches, and immediately in front of it came a first-class, both labelled for the same city. These coaches were fairly well filled, particularly the third-class. In front of the first-class came the last of the four Glasgow sleepers. The train was corridor throughout, and the officials could, and did, pass through it several times during the journey.

It is with the first-class coach that we are principally concerned, and it will be understood from the above that it was placed in between the sleeping-car in front and the third-class behind, the van following immediately behind the third. It had a lavatory at each end and six compartments, the last two, next the third-class, being smokers, the next three non-smoking, and the first, immediately beside the sleeping car, a 'Ladies Only'. The corridors in both it and the third-class coach were on the left-hand side in the direction of travel – that is, the compartments were on the side of the double line.

The night was dark as the train drew out of Euston, for there was no moon and the sky was overcast. As was remembered and commented on afterwards, there had been an unusually long spell of dry weather, and, though it looked like rain earlier in the evening, none fell till the next day, when, about six in the morning, there was a torrential downpour.

As the detectives pointed out later, no weather could have been more unfortunate from their point of view, as, had footmarks been made during the night, the ground would have been too hard to take good impressions, while even such traces as remained would more than likely have been blurred by the rain.

The train ran to time, stopping at Rugby, Crewe and Preston. After leaving the latter station Guard Jones found he had occasion to go forward to speak to a ticket collector in the Edinburgh portion. He accordingly left his van in the rear and passed along the corridor of the third-class carriage adjoining.

At the end of this corridor, beside the vestibule joining it to the first-class, were a lady and gentleman, evidently husband and wife, the lady endeavouring to soothe the cries of a baby she was carrying. Guard Jones addressed some civil remark to the man, who explained that their child had been taken ill, and they had brought it out of their compartment as it was disturbing the other passengers.

With an expression of sympathy, Jones unlocked the two doors across the corridor at the vestibule between the carriages, and, passing on into the first-class coach, re-closed them behind him. They were fitted with spring locks, which became fast on the door shutting.

The corridor of the first-class coach was empty, and as Jones walked down it he observed that the blinds of all the compartments were lowered, with one exception – that of the 'Ladies Only'. In this compartment, which contained three ladies, the light was fully on, and the guard noticed that two out of the three were reading.

Continuing his journey, Jones found that the two doors at the vestibule between the first-class coach and the sleeper were also locked, and he opened them and passed through, shutting them behind him. At the sleeping-car attendant's box, just inside the last of these doors, two car attendants were talking together. One was actually inside the box, the other standing in the corridor. The latter moved aside to let the guard pass, taking up his former position as, after exchanging a few words, Jones moved on.

His business with the ticket collector finished, Guard Jones returned to his van. On this journey he found the same conditions obtaining as on the previous – the two attendants were at the rear end of the sleeping-car, the lady and gentleman with the baby in the front end of the third-class coach, the first-class corridor deserted, and both doors at each end of the latter coach locked. These details, casually remarked at the time, became afterwards of the utmost importance, adding as they did to the mystery in which the tragedy was enveloped.

About an hour before the train was due at Carlisle, while it was passing through the wild moorland country of the Westmorland highlands, the brakes were applied – at first gently, and then with considerable power. Guard Jones, who was examining parcel waybills in the rear end of his van, supposed it to be a signal check, but as such was unusual at this place, he left his work and, walking down the van, lowered the window at the left-hand side and looked out along the train.

The line happened to be in a cutting, and the railway bank for some distance ahead was dimly illuminated by the light from the corridors of the first- and third-class coaches immediately in front of his van. As I have said, the night was dark, and, except for this bit of bank, Jones could see nothing ahead. The railway curved away to the right, so, thinking he might see better from the other side, he crossed the van and looked out of the opposite window, next the up line.

There were no signal lights in view, nor anything to suggest the cause of the slack, but as he ran his eye along the train he saw that something was amiss in the first-class coach. From the window at its rear end figures were leaning, gesticulating wildly, as if to attract attention to some grave and pressing danger. The guard at once ran through the third-class to this coach, and there he found a strange and puzzling state of affairs.

The corridor was still empty, but the centre blind of the rear compartment – that is, the first reached by the guard – had been raised. Through the glass Jones could see that the compartment contained four men. Two were leaning out of the window on the opposite side, and two were fumbling at the latch of the corridor door, as if trying to open it. Jones caught hold of the outside handle to assist, but they pointed in the direction of the adjoining compartment, and the guard, obeying their signs, moved on to the second door.

The centre blind of this compartment had also been pulled

up, though here, again, the door had not been opened. As the guard peered in through the glass he saw that he was in the presence of a tragedy.

Tugging desperately at the handle of the corridor door stood a lady, her face blanched, her eyes starting from her head, and her features frozen into an expression of deadly fear and horror. As she pulled she kept glancing over her shoulder, as if some dreadful apparition lurked in the shadows behind. As Jones sprang forward to open the door his eyes followed the direction of her gaze, and he drew in his breath sharply.

At the far side of the compartment, facing the engine and huddled down in the corner, was the body of a woman. She lay limp and inert, with head tilted back at an unnatural angle into the cushions and a hand hanging helplessly down over the edge of the seat. She might have been thirty years of age, and was dressed in a reddish-brown fur coat with toque to match. But these details the guard hardly glanced at, his attention being riveted to her forehead. There, above the left eyebrow, was a sinister little hole, from which the blood had oozed down the coat and formed a tiny pool on the seat. That she was dead was obvious.

But this was not all. On the seat opposite her lay a man, and, as far as Guard Jones could see, he also was dead.

He apparently had been sitting in the corner seat, and had fallen forward so that his chest lay across the knees of the woman and his head hung down towards the floor. He was all bunched and twisted up — just a shapeless mass in a grey frieze overcoat, with dark hair at the back of what could be seen of his head. But under that head the guard caught the glint of falling drops, while a dark, ominous stain grew on the floor beneath.

Jones flung himself on the door, but it would not move. It stood fixed, an inch open, jammed in some mysterious way, imprisoning the lady with her terrible companions.

As she and the guard strove to force it open, the train came to a standstill. At once it occurred to Jones that he could now enter the compartment from the opposite side.

Shouting to reassure the now almost frantic lady, he turned back to the end compartment, intending to pass through it onto the line and so back to that containing the bodies. But here he was again baffled, for the two men had not succeeded in sliding back their door. He seized the handle to help them, and then he noticed their companions had opened the opposite door and were climbing out onto the permanent way.

It flashed through his mind that an up-train passed about this time, and, fearing an accident, he ran down the corridor to the sleeping-car, where he felt sure he would find a door that would open. That at the near end was free, and he leaped out onto the track. As he passed he shouted to one of the attendants to follow him, and to the other to remain where he was and let no one pass. Then he joined the men who had already alighted, warned them about the up-train, and the four opened the outside door of the compartment in which the tragedy had taken place.

Their first concern was to get the uninjured lady out, and here a difficult and ghastly task awaited them. The door was blocked by the bodies, and its narrowness prevented more than one man from working. Sending the car attendant to search the train for a doctor, Jones clambered up, and, after warning the lady not to look at what he was doing, he raised the man's body and propped it back in the corner seat.

The face was a strong one with clean-shaven but rather coarse features, a large nose, and a heavy jaw. In the neck, just below the right ear, was a bullet hole which, owing to the position of the head, had bled freely. As far as the guard could see, the man was dead. Not without a certain shrinking, Jones raised the feet, first of the man, and then of the woman, and placed them on the seats, thus leaving the floor clear except for its dark, creeping pool. Then, placing his handkerchief over the dead woman's face, he rolled back the end of the carpet to hide its sinister stain.

'Now, ma'am, if you please,' he said; and keeping the lady with her back to the more gruesome object on the opposite seat, he helped her to the open door, from where willing hands assisted her to the ground.

By this time the attendant had found a doctor in the third-class coach, and a brief examination enabled him to pronounce both victims dead. The blinds in the compartment having been drawn down and the outside door locked, the guard called to those passengers who had alighted to resume their seats, with a view to continuing their journey.

The fireman had meantime come back along the train to ascertain what was wrong, and to say the driver was unable completely to release the brake. An examination was therefore made, and the tell-tale disc at the end of the first-class coach was found to be turned, showing that someone in that carriage had pulled the communication chain. This, as is perhaps not generally known, allows air to pass between the train pipe and the atmosphere, thereby gently applying the brake and preventing its complete release. Further investigation showed that the slack of the chain was hanging in the end smoking compartment, indicating that the alarm must have been operated by one of the four men who travelled there. The disc was then turned back to normal, the passengers re-seated, and the train started, after a delay of about fifteen minutes.

Before reaching Carlisle, Guard Jones took the name and address of everyone travelling in the first- and third-class coaches, together with the numbers of their tickets. These coaches, as well as the van, were thoroughly searched, and it was established beyond any doubt that no one was concealed under the seats, in the lavatories, behind luggage, or, in fact, anywhere about them.

One of the sleeping-car attendants having been in the corridor in the rear of the last sleeper from the Preston stop till the completion of this search, and being positive no one except the guard had passed during that time, it was not considered necessary to take the names of the passengers in the sleeping-cars, but the numbers of their tickets were noted.

On arrival at Carlisle the matter was put into the hands of the police. The first-class carriage was shunted off, the doors being locked and sealed, and the passengers who had travelled in it were detained to make their statements. Then began a most careful and searching investigation, as a result of which several additional facts became known.

The first step taken by the authorities was to make an examination of the country surrounding the point at which the train had stopped, in the hope of finding traces of some stranger on the line. The tentative theory was that a murder had been committed and that the murderer had escaped from the train when it stopped, struck across the country, and, gaining some road, had made good his escape.

Accordingly, as soon as it was light, a special train brought a force of detectives to the place, and the railway, as well as a tract of ground on each side of it, were subjected to a prolonged and exhaustive search. But no traces were found. Nothing that a stranger might have dropped was picked up, no footsteps were seen, no marks discovered. As has already been stated, the weather was against the searchers. The drought of the previous days had left the ground hard and unyielding, so that clear impressions were scarcely to be expected, while even such as might have been made were not likely to remain after the downpour of the early morning.

Baffled at this point, the detectives turned their attention to the stations in the vicinity. There were only two within walking distance of the point of the tragedy, and at neither had any stranger been seen. Further, no trains had stopped at either of these stations; indeed, not a single train, either passenger or goods, had stopped anywhere in the neighbourhood since the sleeping-car express went through. If the murderer had left the express, it was, therefore, out of the question that he could have escaped by rail.

The investigators then turned their attention to the country roads and adjoining towns, trying to find the trail – if there was a trail – while it was hot. But here, again, no luck attended their efforts. If there were a murderer, and if he had left the train when it stopped, he had vanished into thin air. No traces of him could anywhere be discovered.

Nor were their researches in other directions much more fruitful.

The dead couple were identified as a Mr and Mrs Horatio Llewelyn, of Gordon Villa, Broad Road, Halifax. Mr Llewelyn was the junior partner of a large firm of Yorkshire ironfounders. A man of five-and-thirty, he moved in good society and had some claim to wealth. He was of kindly though somewhat passionate disposition, and, so far as could be learnt, had not an enemy in the world. His firm was able to show that he had had business appointments in London on the Thursday and in Carlisle on the Friday, so that his travelling by the train in question was quite in accordance with his known plans.

His wife was the daughter of a neighbouring merchant, a pretty girl of some seven-and-twenty. They had been married only a little over a month, and had, in fact, only a week earlier returned from their honeymoon. Whether Mrs Llewelyn had any definite reason for accompanying her husband on the fatal journey could not be ascertained. She also, so far as was known, had no enemy, nor could any motive for the tragedy be suggested.

The extraction of the bullets proved that the same weapon had been used in each case – a revolver of small bore and modern design. But as many thousands of similar revolvers existed, this discovery led to nothing.

Miss Blair-Booth, the lady who had travelled with the Llewelyns, stated she had joined the train at Euston, and occupied one of the seats next to the corridor. A couple of minutes before starting the deceased had arrived, and they sat in the two opposite corners. No other passengers had entered the compartment during the journey, nor had any of the three left it; in fact, except for the single visit of the ticket collector shortly after leaving Euston, the door into the corridor had not been even opened.

Mr Llewelyn was very attentive to his young wife, and they had conversed for some time after starting, then, after consulting Miss Blair-Booth, he had pulled down the blinds and shaded the light, and they had settled down for the night. Miss Blair-Booth had slept at intervals, but each time she wakened she had looked round the compartment, and everything was as before. Then she was suddenly aroused from a doze by a loud explosion close by.

She sprang up, and as she did so a flash came from somewhere near her knee, and a second explosion sounded. Startled and trembling, she pulled the shade off the lamp, and then she noticed a little cloud of smoke just inside the corridor door, which had been opened about an inch, and smelled the characteristic odour of burnt powder. Swinging round, she was in time to see Mr Llewelyn dropping heavily forward across his wife's knees, and then she observed the mark on the latter's forehead and realised they had both been shot.

Terrified, she raised the blind of the corridor door which covered the handle and tried to get out to call assistance. But she could not move the door, and her horror was not diminished when she found herself locked in with what she rightly believed were two dead bodies. In despair she pulled the communication chain, but the train did not appear to stop, and she continued struggling with the door till, after what seemed to her hours, the guard appeared, and she was eventually released.

In answer to a question, she further stated that when her blind went up the corridor was empty, and she saw no one till the guard came.

The four men in the end compartment were members of one party travelling from London to Glasgow. For some time after leaving they had played cards, but, about midnight, they too had pulled down their blinds, shaded their lamp, and composed themselves to sleep. In this case also, no person other than the ticket collector had entered the compartment during the journey. But after leaving Preston the door had been opened. Aroused by the stop, one of the men had eaten some fruit, and having thereby soiled his fingers, had washed them in the lavatory. The door then opened as usual. This man saw no one in the corridor, nor did he notice anything out of the common.

Some time after this all four were startled by the sound of two shots. At first they thought of fog signals, then, realising they were too far from the engine to hear such, they, like Miss Blair-Booth, unshaded their lamp, raised the blind over their corridor door, and endeavoured to leave the compartment. Like her they found themselves unable to open their door, and, like her also, they saw that there was no one in the corridor. Believing something serious had happened, they pulled the communication chain, at the same time lowering the outside window and waving from it in the hope of attracting attention. The chain came down easily as if slack, and this explained the apparent contradiction between Miss Blair-Booth's statement that she had pulled it, and the fact that the slack was found hanging in the end compartment. Evidently the lady had pulled it first, applying the brake, and the second pull had simply transferred the slack from one compartment to the next.

The two compartments in front of that of the tragedy were found to be empty when the train stopped, but in the last of the non-smoking compartments were two gentlemen, and in the 'Ladies Only', three ladies. All these had heard the shots, but so faintly above the noise of the train that the attention of none of them was specially arrested, nor had they attempted any investigation. The gentlemen had not left their compartment or pulled up their blinds between the time the train left Preston and the emergency stop, and could throw no light whatever on the matter.

The three ladies in the end compartment were a mother and two daughters, and had got in at Preston. As they were alighting at Carlisle they had not wished to sleep, so they had left their blinds up and their light unshaded. Two of them were reading, but the third was seated at the corridor side, and this lady stated positively that no one except the guard had passed while they were in the train.

She described his movements – first, towards the engine, secondly, back towards the van, and a third time, running, towards the engine after the train had stopped – so accurately in accord with the other evidence that considerable reliance was placed on her testimony. The stoppage and the guard's haste had aroused her interest, and all three ladies had immediately come out into the corridor, and had remained there till the train proceeded, and all three were satisfied that no one else had passed during that time.

An examination of the doors which had jammed so mysteriously revealed the fact that a small wooden wedge, evidently designed for the purpose, had been driven in between the floor and the bottom of the framing of the door, holding the latter rigid. It was evident therefore that the crime was premeditated, and the details had been carefully worked out beforehand. The most careful search of the carriage failed to reveal any other suspicious object or mark.

On comparing the tickets issued with those held by the passengers, a discrepancy was discovered. All were accounted for except one. A first single for Glasgow had been issued at Euston for the train in question, which had not been collected. The purchaser had therefore either not travelled at all, or had got out at some intermediate station. In either case no demand for a refund had been made.

The collector who had checked the tickets after the train left London believed, though he could not speak positively, that two men had then occupied the non-smoking compartment next to that in which the tragedy had occurred, one of whom held a Glasgow ticket, and the other a ticket for an intermediate station. He could not recollect which station nor could he describe either of the men, if indeed they were there at all.

But the ticket collector's recollection was not at fault, for the police succeeded in tracing one of these passengers, a Dr Hill, who had got out at Crewe. He was able, partially at all events, to account for the missing Glasgow ticket. It appeared that when he joined the train at Euston, a man of about five-and-thirty was already in the compartment. This man had fair hair, blue eyes and a full moustache, and was dressed in dark well-cut clothes. He had no luggage, but only a waterproof and a paper-covered novel. The two travellers had got into conversation, and on the stranger learning that the doctor lived at Crewe, said he was alighting there also, and asked to be recommended to a hotel. He then explained that he had intended to go on to Glasgow and had taken a ticket to that city, but had since decided to break his journey to visit a friend in Chester next day. He asked the doctor if he thought his ticket would be available to complete the journey the following night, and if not, whether he could get a refund.

When they reached Crewe, both these travellers had alighted, and the doctor offered to show his acquaintance the entrance to the Crewe Arms, but the stranger, thanking him, declined, saying he wished to see to his luggage. Dr Hill saw him walking towards the van as he left the platform.

Upon interrogating the staff on duty at Crewe at the time, no one could recall seeing such a man at the van, nor had any enquiries about luggage been made. But as these facts did not come to light until several days after the tragedy, confirmation was hardly to be expected.

A visit to all the hotels in Crewe and Chester revealed the fact that no one in any way resembling the stranger had stayed there, nor could any trace whatever be found of him.

Such were the principal facts made known at the adjourned inquest on the bodies of Mr and Mrs Llewelyn. It was confidently believed that a solution to the mystery would speedily be found, but as day after day passed away without bringing to light any fresh information, public interest began to wane, and became directed into other channels.

But for a time controversy over the affair waxed keen. At first it was argued that it was a case of suicide, some holding that Mr Llewelyn had shot first his wife and then himself; others that both had died by the wife's hand. But this theory had only to be stated to be disproved.

Several persons hastened to point out that not only had the revolver disappeared, but on neither body was there powder blackening, and it was admitted that such a wound could not be self-inflicted without leaving marks from this source. That murder had been committed was therefore clear.

Rebutted on this point, the theorists then argued that Miss Blair-Booth was the assassin. But here again the suggestion was quickly negatived. The absence of motive, her known character and the truth of such of her statements as could be checked were against the idea. The disappearance of the revolver was also in her favour. As it was not in the compartment nor concealed about her person, she could only have rid herself of it out of the window. But the position of the bodies prevented access to the window, and, as her clothes were free from any stain of blood, it was impossible to believe she had moved these grim relics, even had she been physically able.

But the point that finally demonstrated her innocence was the wedging of the corridor door. It was obvious she could not have wedged the door on the outside and then passed through it. The belief was universal that whoever wedged the door fired the shots, and the fact that the former was wedged an inch open strengthened that view, as the motive was clearly to leave a slot through which to shoot.

Lastly, the medical evidence showed that if the Llewelyns were sitting where Miss Blair-Booth stated, and the shots were fired from where she said, the bullets would have entered the bodies from the direction they were actually found to have done.

But Miss Blair-Booth's detractors were loath to recede from the position they had taken up. They stated that of the objections to their theory only one – the wedging of the doors – was overwhelming. And they advanced an ingenious theory to meet it. They suggested that before reaching Preston Miss Blair-Booth had left the compartment, closing the door after her, that she had then wedged it, and that, on stopping at the station, she had passed out through some other compartment, re-entering her own through the outside door.

In answer to this it was pointed out that the gentleman who had eaten the fruit had opened his door *after* the Preston stop, and if Miss Blair-Booth was then shut into her compartment she could not have wedged the other door. That two people should be concerned in the wedging was unthinkable. It was therefore clear that Miss Blair-Booth was innocent, and that some other person had wedged both doors, in order to prevent his operations in the corridor being interfered with by those who would hear the shots.

It was recognised that similar arguments applied to the four men in the end compartment – the wedging of the doors cleared them also.

Defeated on these points the theorists retired from the field. No further suggestions were put forward by the public or the daily press. Even to those behind the scenes the case seemed to become more and more difficult the longer it was pondered.

Each person known to have been present came in turn under the microscopic eye of New Scotland Yard, but each in turn had to be eliminated from suspicion, till it almost seemed proved that no murder could have been committed at all. The prevailing mystification was well summed up by the chief at the Yard in conversation with the inspector in charge of the case.

'A troublesome business, certainly,' said the great man, 'and I admit that your conclusions seem sound. But let us go over it again. There *must* be a flaw somewhere.'

'There must, sir. But I've gone over it and over it till I'm stupid, and every time I get the same result.'

'We'll try once more. We begin, then, with a murder in a railway carriage. We're sure it was a murder, of course?'

'Certain, sir. The absence of the revolver and of powder blackening and the wedging of the doors prove it.'

'Quite. The murder must therefore have been committed by some possibilities in turn. And first, with regard to the searching. Was that efficiently done?'

'Absolutely, sir. I have gone into it with the guard and attendants. No one could have been overlooked.'

'Very good. Taking first, then, those who were in the carriage. There were six compartments. In the first were the four men, and in the second Miss Blair-Booth. Are you satisfied these were innocent?'

'Perfectly, sir. The wedging of the doors eliminated them.'

'So I think. The third and fourth compartments were empty, but in the fifth there were two gentlemen. What about them?'

'Well, sir, you know who they were. Sir Gordon McClean, the great engineer, and Mr Silas Hemphill, the professor of Aberdeen University. Both utterly beyond suspicion.'

'But, as you know, Inspector, *no one* is beyond suspicion in a case of this kind.'

'I admit it, sir, and therefore I made careful enquiries about them. But I only confirmed my opinion.'

'From enquiries I also have made I feel sure you are right. That brings us to the last compartment, the "Ladies Only". What about those three ladies?'

'The same remarks apply. Their characters are also beyond suspicion, and, as well as that, the mother is elderly and timid, and couldn't brazen out a lie. I question if the daughters could either. I made enquiries all the same, and found not the slightest ground for suspicion.'

'The corridors and lavatories were empty?'

'Yes, sir.'

'Then everyone found in the coach when the train stopped may be definitely eliminated?'

'Yes. It is quite impossible it could have been any that we have mentioned.'

'Then the murderer must have left the coach?'

'He must; and that's where the difficulty comes in.'

'I know, but let us proceed. Our problem then really becomes – *how* did he leave the coach?'

'That's so, sir, and I have never been against anything stiffer.'

The chief paused in thought, as he absently selected and lit another cigar. At last he continued:

'Well, at any rate, it is clear he did not go through the roof or the floor, or any part of the fixed framing or sides. Therefore he must have gone in the usual way – through a door. Of these, there is one at each end and six at each side.

He therefore went through one of these fourteen doors. Are you agreed, Inspector?'

'Certainly, sir.'

'Very good. Take the ends first. The vestibule doors were locked?'

'Yes, sir, at both ends of the coach. But I don't count that much. An ordinary carriage key opened them and the murderer would have had one.'

'Quite. Now, just go over again our reason for thinking he did not escape to the sleeper.'

'Before the train stopped, sir, Miss Bintley, one of the three in the "Ladies Only", was looking out into the corridor, and the two sleeper attendants were at the near end of their coach. After the train stopped, all three ladies were in the corridor, and one attendant was at the sleeper vestibule. All these persons swear most positively that no one but the guard passed between Preston and the searching of the carriage.'

'What about these attendants? Are they reliable?'

'Wilcox has seventeen years' service, and Jeffries six, and both bear excellent characters. Both, naturally, came under suspicion of the murder, and I made the usual investigation. But there is not a scrap of evidence against them, and I am satisfied they are all right.'

'It certainly looks as if the murderer did not escape towards the sleeper.'

'I am positive of it. You see, sir, we have the testimony of two separate lots of witnesses, the ladies and the attendants. It is out of the question that these parties would agree to deceive the police. Conceivably one or other might, but not both.'

'Yes, that seems sound. What, then, about the other end –
the third-class end?'

'At that end,' replied the inspector, 'were Mr and Mrs
Smith with their sick child. They were in the corridor close
by the vestibule door, and no one could have passed without
their knowledge. I had the child examined, and its illness
was genuine. The parents are quiet persons, of exemplary
character, and again quite beyond suspicion. When they said
no one but the guard had passed I believed them. However,
I was not satisfied with that, and I examined every person
that travelled in the third-class coach, and established two
things: first, that no one was in it at the time it was searched
who had not travelled in it from Preston; and secondly, that
no one except the Smiths had left any of the compartments
during the run between Preston and the emergency stop.
That proves beyond question that no one left the first-class
coach for the third after the tragedy.'

'What about the guard himself?'

'The guard is also a man of good character, but he is out
of it, because he was seen by several passengers as well as
the Smiths running through the third-class after the brakes
were applied.'

'It is clear, then, the murderer must have got out through
one of the twelve side doors. Take those on the compartment
side first. The first, second, fifth and sixth compartments
were occupied, therefore he could not have passed through
them. That leaves the third and fourth doors. Could he have
left by either of these?'

The inspector shook his head.

'No, sir,' he answered, 'that is equally out of the question.

You will recollect that two of the four men in the end compartment were looking out along the train from a few seconds after the murder until the stop. It would not have been possible to open a door and climb out onto the footboard without being seen by them. Guard Jones also looked out at that side of the van and saw no one. After the stop these same two men, as well as others, were on the ground, and all agree that none of these doors were opened at any time.'

'H'm,' mused the chief, 'that also seems conclusive, and it brings us definitely to the doors on the corridor side. As the guard arrived on the scene comparatively early, the murderer must have got out while the train was running at a fair speed. He must therefore have been clinging onto the outside of the coach while the guard was in the corridor working at the sliding doors. When the train stopped all attention was concentrated on the opposite, or compartment, side, and he could easily have dropped down and made off. What do you think of that theory, Inspector?'

'We went into that pretty thoroughly, sir. It was first objected that the blinds of the first and second compartments were raised too soon to give him time to get out without being seen. But I found this was not valid. At least fifteen seconds must have elapsed before Miss Blair-Booth and the men in the end compartment raised their blinds, and that would easily have allowed him to lower the window, open the door, pass out, raise the window, shut the door, and crouch down on the footboard out of sight. I estimate also that nearly thirty seconds passed before Guard Jones looked out of the van at that side. As far as time goes he could have done what you suggest. But another thing shows he didn't. It appears that when Jones ran through the third-class coach, while the train was stopping, Mr Smith, the man with the sick child, wondering what was wrong, attempted to follow him into the first-class. But the door slammed after the guard before the other could reach it, and, of course, the spring lock held it fast. Mr Smith therefore lowered the end corridor window and looked out ahead, and he states positively no one was on the footboard of the first-class. To see how far Mr Smith could be sure of this, on a dark night we ran the same carriage, lighted in the same way, over the same part of the line, and we found a figure crouching on the footboard was clearly visible from the window. It showed a dark mass against the lighted side of the cutting. When we remember that Mr Smith was specially looking out for something abnormal, I think we may accept his evidence.'

'You are right. It is convincing. And, of course, it is supported by the guard's own testimony. He also saw no one when he looked out of his van.'

'That is so, sir. And we found a crouching figure was visible from the van also, owing to the same cause – the lighted bank.'

'And the murderer could not have got out while the guard was passing through the third-class?'

'No, because the corridor blinds were raised before the guard looked out.'

The chief frowned.

'It is certainly puzzling,' he mused. There was silence for some moments, and then he spoke again.

'Could the murderer, immediately after firing the shots, have concealed himself in a lavatory and then, during the excitement of the stop, have slipped out unperceived through one of these corridor doors and, dropping on the line, moved quietly away?'

'No, sir, we went into that also. If he had hidden in a lavatory he could not have got out again. If he had gone towards the third-class the Smiths would have seen him, and the first-class corridor was under observation during the entire time from the arrival of the guard till the search. We have proved the ladies entered the corridor *immediately* the guard passed their compartment, and two of the four men in the end smoker were watching through their door till considerably after the ladies had come out.'

Again silence reigned while the chief smoked thoughtfully.

'The coroner had some theory, you say?' he said at last.

'Yes, sir. He suggested the murderer might have, immediately after firing, got out by one of the doors on the corridor side – probably the end one – and from there climbed on the outside of the coach to some place from which he could not be seen from a window, dropping to the ground when the train stopped. He suggested the roof, the buffers, or the lower step. This seemed likely at first sight, and I tried therefore the experiment. But it was no good. The roof was out of the question. It was one of those high curved roofs – not a flat clerestory – and there was no hand-hold at the edge above the doors. The buffers were equally inaccessible. From the handle and guard of the end door to that above the buffer on the corner of the coach was seven feet two inches. That is to say, a man could not reach from one to the other, and there was nothing he could hold on to while passing along the step. The lower step was not possible either. In the first place it was divided – there was only a short step beneath each door – not a continuous board like the upper one – so that no one could pass along the lower while holding on to the upper, and secondly, I couldn't imagine anyone climbing down there, and knowing that the first platform they came to would sweep him off.'

'That is to say, Inspector, you have proved the murderer was in the coach at the time of the crime, that he was not in it when it was searched, and that he did not leave it in the interval. I don't know that that is a very creditable conclusion.'

'I know, sir. I regret it extremely, but that's the difficulty I have been up against from the start.'

The chief laid his hand on his subordinate's shoulder.

'It won't do,' he said kindly. It really won't do. You try again. Smoke over it, and I'll do the same, and come in and see me again tomorrow.'

But the conversation had really summed up the case justly. My Lady Nicotine brought no inspiration, and, as time passed without bringing to light any further facts, interest gradually waned till at last the affair took its place among the long list of unexplained crimes in the annals of New Scotland Yard.

And now I come to the singular coincidence referred to earlier whereby I, an obscure medical practitioner, came to learn the solution of this extraordinary mystery. With the case itself I had no connection, the details just given being taken from the official reports made at the time, to which I was allowed access in return for the information I brought. The affair happened in this way.

One evening just four weeks ago, as I lit my pipe after a

long and tiring day, I received an urgent summons to the principal inn of the little village near which I practised. A motorcyclist had collided with a car at a crossroads and had been picked up terribly injured. I saw almost at a glance that nothing could be done for him; in fact, his life was a matter of a few hours. He asked coolly how it was with him, and, in accordance with my custom in such cases, I told him, enquiring was there anyone he would like sent for. He looked me straight in the eyes and replied:

'Doctor, I want to make a statement. If I tell it to you will you keep it to yourself while I live and then inform the proper authorities and the public?'

'Why, yes,' I answered; 'but shall I not send for some of your friends or a clergyman?'

'No,' he said, 'I have no friends, and I have no use for parsons. You look a white man; I would rather tell you.'

I bowed and fixed him up as comfortably as possible, and he began, speaking slowly in a voice hardly above a whisper.

'I shall be brief for I feel my time is short. You remember some few years ago a Mr Horatio Llewelyn and his wife were murdered in a train on the North-Western some fifty miles south of Carlisle?'

I dimly remembered the case.

'"The sleeping-car express mystery", the papers called it?' I asked.

'That's it,' he replied. 'They never solved the mystery and they never got the murderer. But he's going to pay now. I am he.'

I was horrified at the cool, deliberate way he spoke. Then I remembered that he was fighting death to make his confession and that, whatever my feelings, it was my business to hear and record it while yet there was time. I therefore sat down and said as gently as I could:

'Whatever you tell me I shall note carefully, and at the proper time shall inform the police.'

His eyes, which had watched me anxiously, showed relief.

'Thank you. I shall hurry. My name is Hubert Black, and I live at 24, Westbury Gardens, Hove. Until ten years and two months ago I lived at Bradford, and there I made the acquaintance of what I thought was the best and most wonderful girl on God's earth – Miss Gladys Wentworth. I was poor, but she was well-off. I was diffident about approaching her, but she encouraged me till at last I took my courage in both hands and proposed. She agreed to marry me, but made it a condition our engagement was to be kept secret for a few days. I was so mad about her I would have agreed to anything she wanted, so I said nothing, though I could hardly behave like a sane man from joy.

'Some time before this I had come across Llewelyn, and he had been very friendly, and had seemed to like my company. One day we met Gladys, and I introduced him. I did not know till later that he had followed up the acquaintanceship.

'A week after my acceptance there was a big dance at Halifax. I was to have met Gladys there, but at the last moment I had a wire that my mother was seriously ill, and I had to go. On my return I got a cool little note from Gladys saying she was sorry, but our engagement had been a mistake, and I must consider it at an end. I made a few enquiries, and then I learnt what had been done. Give me some stuff, doctor; I'm going down.'

I poured out some brandy and held it to his lips.

'That's better,' he said, continuing with gasps and many pauses: 'Llewelyn, I found out, had been struck by Gladys for some time. He knew I was friends with her, and so he made up to me. He wanted the introduction I was fool enough to give him, as well as the chances of meeting her he would get with me. Then he met her when he knew I was at my work, and made hay while the sun shone. Gladys spotted what he was after, but she didn't know if he was serious. Then I proposed, and she thought she would hold me for fear the bigger fish would get off. Llewelyn was wealthy, you understand. She waited till the ball, then she hooked him, and I went overboard. Nice, wasn't it?'

I did not reply, and the man went on:

'Well, after that I just went mad. I lost my head and went to Llewelyn, but he laughed in my face. I felt I wanted to knock his head off, but the butler happened by, so I couldn't go on and finish him then. I needn't try to describe the hell I went through – I couldn't, anyway. But I was blind mad, and lived only for revenge. And then I got it. I followed them till I got a chance, and then I killed them. I shot them in that train. I shot her first and then, as he woke and sprang up, I got him too.'

The man paused.

'Tell me the details,' I asked; and after a time he went on in a weaker voice:

'I had worked out a plan to get them in a train, and had followed them all through their honeymoon, but I never got a chance till then. This time the circumstances fell out to suit. I was behind him at Euston and heard him book to

Carlisle, so I booked to Glasgow. I got into the next compartment. There was a talkative man there, and I tried to make a sort of alibi for myself by letting him think I would get out at Crewe. I did get out, but I got in again, and travelled on in the same compartment with the blinds down. No one knew I was there. I waited till we got to the top of Shap, for I thought I could get away easier in a thinly populated country. Then, when the time came, I fixed the compartment doors with wedges, and shot them both. I left the train and got clear of the railway, crossing the country till I came on a road. I hid during the day and walked at night till after dark on the second evening I came to Carlisle. From there I went by rail quite openly. I was never suspected.'

He paused, exhausted, while the Dread Visitor hovered closer.

'Tell me,' I said, 'just a word. How did you get out of the train?'

He smiled faintly.

'Some more of your stuff,' he whispered; and when I had given him a second dose of brandy he went on feebly and with long pauses which I am not attempting to reproduce:

'I had worked the thing out beforehand. I thought if I could get out on the buffers while the train was running and before the alarm was raised, I should be safe. No one looking out of the windows could see me, and when the train stopped, as I knew it soon would, I could drop down and make off. The difficulty was to get from the corridor to the buffers. I did it like this:

'I had brought about sixteen feet of fine, brown silk cord, and the same length of thin silk rope. When I got out at Crewe

I moved to the corner of the coach and stood close to it by way of getting shelter to light a cigarette. Without anyone seeing what I was up to I slipped the end of the cord through the bracket handle above the buffers. Then I strolled to the nearest door, paying out the cord, but holding on to its two ends. I pretended to fumble at the door as if it was stiff to open, but all the time I was passing the cord through the handle-guard, and knotting the ends together. If you've followed me you'll understand this gave me a loop of fine silk connecting the handles at the corner and the door. It was the colour of the carriage, and was nearly invisible. Then I took my seat again.

'When the time came to do the job, I first wedged the corridor doors. Then I opened the outside window and drew in the end of the cord loop and tied the end of the rope to it. I pulled one side of the cord loop and so got the rope pulled through the corner bracket handle and back again to the window. Its being silk made it run easily, and without marking the bracket. Then I put an end of the rope through the handle-guard, and after pulling it tight, knotted the ends together. This gave me a loop of rope tightly stretched from the door to the corner.

'I opened the door and then pulled up the window. I let the door close up against a bit of wood I had brought. The wind kept it to, and the wood prevented it from shutting.

'Then I fired. As soon as I saw that both were hit I got outside. I kicked away the wood and shut the door. Then with the rope for handrail I stepped along the footboard to the buffers. I cut both the cord and the rope and drew them after me, and shoved them in my pocket. This removed all traces.

'When the train stopped I slipped down on the ground. The people were getting out at the other side so I had only to creep along close to the coaches till I got out of their light, then I climbed up the bank and escaped.'

The man had evidently made a desperate effort to finish, for as he ceased speaking his eyes closed, and in a few minutes he fell into a state of coma which shortly preceded his death.

After communicating with the police I set myself to carry out his second injunction, and this statement is the result.

The Music Room

Sapper

'I'm afraid I must be terribly materialistic and dull, my dear Anne. I quite agree with you that the house ought to have a ghost, and if I could I'd order one from Harridges. But the prosaic fact remains that so far as I know we just aren't honoured.'

Sir John Crawsham smiled at the girl on his right and helped himself to a second glass of port.

'We've got, I believe, a secret passage of sorts,' he continued. 'I've never bothered to look for it myself, but the legend goes that Charles the First lay hidden in it for two or three days. The only trouble about that is, that if His Majesty had hidden in all the secret rooms he is reputed to have stayed in he'd never have had time to do anything else.'

'We must have a hunt for it one day, Uncle John,' sang out his nephew David from the other end of the table.

'With all the pleasure in the world, my dear boy. I've got

a bit of doggerel about it somewhere, which I'll look up after dinner.'

'How long have you had the house, Sir John?' asked Ronald Standish.

'Two months. Incidentally, Standish, though I can't supply a ghost, I can put up a very strange story which is more or less in your line of country.'

'Really,' said Ronald. 'What is it?'

Sir John pushed the decanter to his left.

'It happened about forty years ago,' he began. 'At the time the house was empty; the tenants were abroad, the servants had either been dismissed or put on board wages. The keys were with the lodge-keeper, and two or three times a week he used to come up to open the windows and generally see that everything was all right. Well, one morning he arrived as usual and proceeded to unlock the doors of all the rooms, according to his ordinary routine. Until, to his great surprise, he came to the music room and found that the key was missing. The door was locked but there was no key.

'He searched on the floor, thinking it might have fallen out of the keyhole; no sign of it. And so after a while he went outside, got a ladder, and climbed up to look through the mullioned windows. And there, lying in the middle of the floor, he saw the body of a man.

'The windows in that room are of the small diamond-paned type and are not easy to see through. But Jobson — that was the lodge-keeper's name — realised at once that something was badly amiss and got hold of the police, who proceeded to break open the door. And there an appalling sight confronted them.

'Stretched on his back in the middle of the room was a dead man. But it was the manner of his death that made the sight so terrible. The lower part of his face had literally been battered into a pulp; the assault must have been one of unbelievable ferocity. I say assault advisedly, since it was obvious at once that there could be no question of suicide or accident. It was murder, and a particularly brutal one at that. But when they'd got that far, they found things weren't so easy.

'From the doctor's examination it appeared that the man had been dead for about thirty-six hours. Jobson had not been to the house the preceding day, and so it was clear that the crime had been committed two nights before the body was found. But how had the murderer escaped? The door, as I've told you, was locked on the inside, which showed that the key had been deliberately taken from the outside and placed on the in. The windows were all bolted, and a very short examination proved that it was impossible to fasten them from outside the house. Therefore the murderer could not have escaped through a window and shut it after him. How, then, had he escaped?

'Wait a moment!' Sir John laughed. 'I know what you're all going to say. Through the secret passage, of course. All I can tell you is that the most exhaustive search failed to reveal one. Short of actually pulling down the walls, they did everything they possibly could, so I gathered from the man who told me the yarn.'

'And no trace of any weapon was found?' remarked Ronald.

'Not a sign. But apparently, from the injuries sustained, it must have been something like a crowbar.'

'Was the dead man identified?' I asked.

'No. That was another strange feature of the case. He had no letters or papers on him, and his clothes proved to have been bought in a big ready-made shop in Birmingham. They found the assistant who had served him some weeks previously, but he was of no help. The man had paid on the spot and taken the clothes away with him. And that, I'm afraid, is all that I can do for you in the ghost line,' he finished with a smile.

'Did the police have no theory at all?' asked Ronald.

'They had a theory right enough,' said Sir John. 'Burglary was at the bottom of it; there is some vague rumour that a lot of old gold plate is hidden somewhere in the house. At any rate, the police believed that two men broke in to look for it, bringing with them a crowbar in case it should be necessary to smash down the walls. They then quarrelled, and one of them bashed the other in the face with it, killing him on the spot. And then somehow or other the murderer got away.'

Sir John pushed back his chair.

'After which gruesome contribution to the evening's hilarity,' he remarked, 'who is for a game of slosh?'

There were a dozen of us altogether in the house party and everyone knew everyone else fairly intimately. Our host, a good-looking man in the early fifties, was a bachelor, and his sister Mary Crawsham kept house for him. He was a man of considerable wealth, being one of the partners in Crawsham's Cable Works. The other two were his nephews, David and Michael, sons of the late Sir Wilfred Crawsham, John's elder brother. He had died of pneumonia five years previously, and when his will was read it was found that he had left his share of the business equally to his two sons, who were to be automatically taken into partnership with their uncle.

As a result, the two young men found themselves at a comparatively early age in the pleasant possession of a very large income. Wilfred's share had been considerably larger than his brother's, and so, even when it was split into two, each half was but little less than Sir John's portion. Fortunately, neither of them was of the type that is spoiled by wealth, and two nicer fellows it would have been hard to meet. David was the elder and quieter of the two! Michael — a harum-scarum youth, though quite shrewd when it came to business — spent most of his spare time proposing to Anne Horley, who had started the ghost conversation at dinner.

The party was by way of being a housewarming. Though Sir John had actually had the house for two months, the decorators had only just moved out finally. Extra bathrooms had been installed and the whole place had been modernised. But the work had been done well and the atmosphere of the place had been kept — particularly on the ground floor, where, so far as was possible, everything was as it had been when the house was built.

And especially was this true of the room of the mysterious murder — the music room, into which everyone had automatically trooped after dinner. It possessed a lofty ceiling from which there hung in the centre a large and immensely heavy chandelier. Personally, I thought it hideous, but I gathered it was genuine and valuable. It had been wired for electricity, but the main lighting effect came from lamps dotted about the room. A grand piano — Mary Crawsham was no mean performer – stood not far from the huge fireplace, on each side of which were inglenooks with their original panelling. The chairs, though in keeping, could be sat on without getting cramp; there was no carpet on the floor, but several valuable Persian rugs. Opposite the fireplace was the musicians' gallery, reached by an old oak staircase. Facing the door were the high windows, through which Jobson had peered nearly half a century ago and seen what lay in the room.

'The bloodstain is renewed every week, my dear,' said Sir John jocularly to one of the girls.

'But where exactly was the body, Uncle John?' cried Michael.

'From what I gather, right in the centre of the room. Of course, it was furnished very differently then, but there was a clear space in the middle and that was where he was lying.'

'What do you make of it, Ronald?' said David.

'Good Heavens! My dear fellow, don't ask me to solve the mystery,' laughed Standish. 'Things of that sort are hard enough, even when you've got all the clues red hot. But when they're forty years old—'

'Still, you must have some idea,' persisted Anne Horley.

'You flatter me, Anne. And I'm afraid that the only solution I can see might spoil it as well as solve it. Providing everything was exactly as Sir John told us – and you must remember it took place a long time ago – I think that the police theory is almost certainly correct as far as it goes.'

'But how could the man get away?'

'I am quite sure they knew how he got away, but that part has been allowed to drop so as to increase the mystery. Through the door.'

'But it was locked on the inside.'

Ronald smiled.

'I should say it would take a skilled man with the right implement five minutes at the very most to lock that door from the outside, the key being on the inside. Which brings us to an interesting point. Why should he have troubled to do so? He had just killed his pal; so his first instinct would be to get away as fast as he could. Why, therefore, did he delay even five minutes? Why not lock the door from the outside and put the key in his pocket? He can't have been concerned with staging a nice mystery for future owners of the house; his sole worry at the moment must have been to hop it as rapidly as possible.'

He lit a cigarette.

'You know, little things of that sort always annoy me until I can get, at any rate, a possible solution. Why do laundries invariably send back double-cuffed shirts with the holes for the links at least an inch apart? Why do otherwise sane people persist in believing that placing a poker upright in front of a fire causes it to draw up?'

'But of course it does,' cried Anne indignantly.

'Only, my angel, because at long last you leave the fire alone and cease to poke it.' He dodged a book thrown at his head, and continued. 'Why did that man take the trouble to do what he did? What was in his mind? What possible purpose did he think he was serving? That, to my mind, Sir John, is the really interesting part of your problem. But then I'm afraid I'm a base materialist.'

'Then you don't think there is a secret passage at all?' said Michael.

'I won't say that. But I think if there had been one leading out of this room, the police would have found it.'

'Well, I think you're quite wrong,' remarked Anne scornfully. 'In fact, you almost deserve to be addressed as my dear Watson. What happened is pathetically obvious to anyone except a half-wit. These two men came for the gold plate. They locked the door to ensure they should not be disturbed. Then they searched for the secret passage and found it. There it was, yawning in front of them. At the other end – wealth. On which bright thought Eustace – he's the murderer – sloshes Clarence in the meat trap, so as to get a double share, and legs it along the passage. He finds the gold, and suddenly gets all hit up with an idea. He will leave the house by the other end of the passage. So he goes back; shuts the secret door into this room, and hops it the other way. What about that, my children?'

'Bravo!' cried Ronald, amid a general chorus of applause. 'It's an uncommonly good solution, Anne. It gets rid of my difficulty, and if there is a secret passage I wouldn't be at all surprised if you aren't right.'

'If! My poor child, what you lack is feminine intuition. Had women been in charge of this case it would have been solved thirty-nine years and eleven months ago. I despair of your sex. Come on, children: let's go and dance. I'm tired of ancient corpses.'

The party trooped out into the hall, and Ronald strolled along the wall under the musicians' gallery, tapping the panelling.

'All sounds solid enough, doesn't it?' he remarked. 'They certainly didn't go in for jerry-building in those days, Sir John.'

'You're right,' answered our host. 'Each one of these walls is about three feet thick. I was amazed when I saw the workmen doing some plumbing upstairs before we moved in.' He switched out the lights and we joined the others in the hall, where dancing to the wireless had already started. And as I stood idly watching by the fireplace, and sensing the comfortable wealth of it all, I found myself wishing that I was a partner in Crawsham's Cable Works. I said as much to David, who looked at me, so I thought, a little queerly.

'I wouldn't say it to everybody, Bob,' he remarked, 'but I confess I'm a trifle surprised at things. I'd heard all about the new house, but I did not expect anything quite like this. Crawsham's Cable Works, old boy, have not been entirely immune from the general slump, though we haven't been hit so hard as most people. But that is for your ears only.'

'He's probably landed a packet in gold mines,' I said.

'Probably,' he agreed with a laugh. 'Don't think I'm accusing my reverend uncle of robbing the till. But this ain't a house: it's a ruddy mansion. However, I gather the shooting is excellent, so more power to his elbow. Which reminds me that it's an early start tomorrow, and I've got to see him on a spot of business. Night, night, Bob. That cup stuff is Aunt Mary's own hell-brew. I think she puts ink in it. As the road signs say – you have been warned.'

Which was the last time I saw David Crawsham alive.

Even now, after a considerable lapse of time, I can still feel the stunning shock of the tragedy that took place that night. Big Ben had sounded: National had closed down, and a general drift bedwards took place. Personally, I was asleep almost as soon as my head touched the pillow, only to awake a few seconds later, so it seemed to me, with the sound of a heavy crash reverberating in my ears. For a while I lay listening. Had I dreamed it? Then a door opened and footsteps went past my room. I switched on the light and looked at my watch: it was half past two.

Another door opened and I heard voices. Then a shout in Sir John's voice. I got up and, slipping on a dressing gown, went out. Below I could hear Sir John talking agitatedly to someone, and as Ronald came out of his room, one sentence came up distinctly.

'For God's sake keep the women away!'

I followed Ronald down the stairs: Sir John was standing outside the music room in his dressing gown, talking to the white-faced butler.

'Ring up the doctor at once, and the police,' he was saying, and then he saw us.

'What on earth has happened?' asked Ronald.

'David,' cried his uncle. 'The chandelier has fallen on him.'

'What?' shouted Ronald, and darted into the music room.

In a welter of gold arms and shattered glass the chandelier lay in the centre of the floor, and underneath it sprawled a motionless figure in evening clothes.

'Lift it off him,' said Ronald quietly, and between us we heaved the thing clear. And a glance was sufficient to show that nothing could be done: David was dead. His shirt-front and collar were saturated with blood; his face was crushed almost beyond recognition. And one hand was nearly severed at the wrist, so deep was the cut in it.

'Poor devil,' muttered Ronald, covering up his face.

'Somebody had better break it gently to Michael. Keep everybody out, Bob. Ah! here is Michael.'

'What is it?' cried the younger brother. 'What's happened?'

'Steady, old man,' said Ronald. 'There's been a bad accident. The chandelier fell on David and crushed him.'

'He's dead?'

'Yes, Michael, I'm afraid he is. I wouldn't look if I were you; it'll do no good.'

'But in God's name how did it happen?' he cried wildly. 'What on earth was the old chap doing here at this time of night? He was with you when I went to bed, Uncle John.'

'I know he was,' said Sir John. 'We sat on talking over that tender for about half an hour, and then I went to bed, leaving him in my study. He said he would turn out the lights, and I can tell you no more. I fell asleep, until the frightful crash woke me up. I came down and found this. For some reason or other he must have been in here: he said something jokingly about the secret passage. And then this happened. Of all the incredible pieces of bad luck—'

Sir John was nearly distraught.

'I'll have that damned contractor ruined for this,' he went on. 'He should be sent to prison. Don't you agree, Standish?'

There was no answer and, glancing at Ronald, I saw that he was staring at the body with a look of perplexed amazement on his face.

'What's that?' he said, coming out of his reverie. 'The contractor. I agree; quite scandalous.'

He walked round and examined the top of the chandelier.

'Funny a chain wasn't used to hold it,' he remarked. 'Though this rope is obviously new, and should have been strong enough. What room is immediately above here, Sir John?'

'It's going to be my bedroom, but the fools put down the wrong flooring. I wanted parquet, so I made 'em take it up again. They're coming to do it next week.'

'I see,' said Ronald, and once again his eyes came back to the body with a look of absorbed interest in them. Then abruptly he left the room, and when I went into the hall, where the whole party were talking in hushed whispers, he was nowhere to be seen.

'It's that room, Mr Leyton,' said Miss Crawsham to me between her sobs. 'There's tragedy in it; something devilish. I know it. Poor Michael! He's gone all to pieces. He adored his brother.'

And certainly the pall of tragedy brooded over the house. It was the suddenness of it; the stupid waste of a brilliant young life from such a miserable cause.

The doctor came, though we all knew it was merely a matter of form. I heard his report to Sir John.

'A terrible affair,' he said gravely. 'I must offer you my deepest sympathy. It is, of course, clear what happened: so clear that it is hardly necessary for me to say it. Your nephew was standing under the chandelier when the rope broke. He must have heard something and looked up. And the base of the chandelier struck him in the face. I am sure it will be a comfort to you to know, Sir John, that death must have been instantaneous. Of that I am certain. I shall, of course, wait for the police.'

And at that moment I felt a hand on my arm. Ronald was standing beside me.

'Come into the billiard room, Bob,' he said in a low voice.

I followed him and threw a log on the dying fire. Then in some surprise I looked at him. Rarely had I seen him more serious.

'That doctor is a fool,' he said abruptly.

'Why? What makes you say so?' I asked, amazed. 'Don't you agree with him?'

For a space he walked up and down the room, his hands in the pockets of his dressing gown. Then he halted in front of me.

'David's death was instantaneous all right; I agree there. But he wasn't standing underneath the chandelier when it fell.'

'What was he doing then?'

'He was lying on the floor.'

'Lying! What under the sun do you mean? Why was he lying on the floor?'

'Because,' he said quietly, 'he was dead already.'

I stared at him in complete bewilderment.

'How do you make that out?' I said at length.

'That very deep cut in his hand,' he answered. 'Had he received that at the same time as he received the blow in the face it would have bled profusely, just as his face did. Whereas, in actual fact, it hardly bled at all. There are some other scratches, too, obviously caused by breaking glass which show no signs of blood. And so I say, Bob, that without a shadow of doubt, David Crawsham was already dead when the chandelier fell on him.'

'Then what killed him?'

'I don't know,' said Ronald gravely. 'But it is a significant point that if you eliminate the chandelier, David's death is identical with that of the man forty years ago. Both found lying in the centre of the room with their faces bashed in.'

'Do you mean that you think there's something in the room?'

'I don't know what to think, Bob. If by something you mean some supernatural agency, I emphatically do *not* think. That wound was caused by a very material weapon, wielded by very material power.'

'You think it quite impossible that for some strange reason the wound in his wrist did not bleed? That all the blood that flowed came from his face?'

'I think it quite impossible, Bob, that those two wounds were administered simultaneously.'

'His face would have been hit first,' I pointed out.

'By the split fraction of a second. Damn it, man, his hand was almost severed from his arm. He ought to have bled there like a pig.'

'In that case what are you going to do about it?'

He again began to pace up and down the room.

'Look here, Bob,' he said at length, 'as I see it, there are two possible alternatives. The first is that somebody murdered David by hitting him in the face with some heavy weapon. He then placed the body on the floor under the chandelier and, going up above to the room without floorboards, deliberately cut the rope.'

'But the rope wasn't cut,' I cried. 'It was all frayed.'

'My dear man,' he answered irritably, 'use your common sense. Would any man be such a congenital fool as not to fray out the two ends after he'd cut the rope? The whole thing must appear to be an accident. The top end which I went and had a look at is frayed just like the bit on the chandelier. But that proved nothing. It's what you would expect to find if it was an accident or if it wasn't. That's the first alternative. The second is, I confess, a tough 'un to swallow. It is that something – don't ask me what – struck David in the face with sufficient force to kill him. He fell where we found him, and later the rope supporting the chandelier broke, and the thing crashed down on him.'

'But if something hit him, not wielded by a human agency, that something must still be in the room,' I cried.

'I told you it was a tough 'un,' he said. And the first isn't too easy either. The blow wasn't on the back of the head. He must have seen it coming; he must have seen the murderer winding himself up to deliver it. Can we seriously believe that he stood stock still waiting to be hit? It's a teaser, Bob, a regular teaser.'

'Well, old man,' I remarked. 'I have the greatest respect for your judgement, but I can't help thinking that in this case you're wrong. Who could possibly want to murder David? And though I realise the force of your argument about the wound in his wrist, it's surely easier to accept the doctor's solution than either of yours.'

'Very much easier,' he agreed shortly, and led the way back into the hall. The police had arrived and were taking notes in readiness for the inquest; the doctor had already left. The women had all gone back to their rooms. Only the men, with the exception of Michael, still stood about aimlessly.

I wondered if Ronald was going to say to the police what he had said to me, but he did not mention it. He gave his name, as I did mine — but as they obviously agreed with the doctor that the whole thing was an accident, the proceedings were merely a matter of routine.

At length they departed, having carried David's body to his room. And after a while we drifted away. The first streaks of dawn were beginning to show, and for a time I stood by the window smoking. And when at last I lay down it was not with any thought of sleeping. But finally I did doze off, to awake in a muck sweat from a nightmare in which some huge black object had come rushing at me out of space in the music room.

The result of the inquest was a foregone conclusion. The building contractor produced figures to prove that the rope which had been used was strong enough to carry a weight twice as great as that of the chandelier, and that therefore he could not be held to blame for what must evidently have been a hidden flaw.

And so a verdict of accidental death was brought in, and in due course David Crawsham was buried. Only his aunt remained unconvinced, maintaining that there was a malevolent spirit in the room who had cut the rope deliberately. And Ronald. He did not say anything; on the face of it he acquiesced with the coroner's finding. But I knew he was convinced in his own mind that the verdict was wrong. And often during the months that followed I would find him with knitted brows staring into vacancy as he puffed at his pipe. But at last in the stress of other work he forgot it, until one day Michael caught Anne at the right moment and they became engaged. Which was the cause of our being again invited by Sir John to a party to celebrate the event.

The guests, save for ourselves and Anne, were all different from those who had been there when the tragedy occurred, and somewhat naturally no mention was made of it. The music room was in general use, but there was one alteration. The chandelier had been removed.

'My sister insisted on it,' said Sir John to me. And I think she was right. A pity though in some ways; of its type it was very fine.'

'Have you got any farther with finding the secret passage?' I asked.

He shook his head.

'No. Since the poor boy's death I haven't given the matter a second thought. What a ghastly night that was. I believe I've still got the paper somewhere,' he said vaguely.

But one thing was clear; whatever Sir John had done, Ronald was giving it several second thoughts. Returning to the scene of the accident had brought the whole matter back to his mind, and I could see he was still as dissatisfied as ever.

'Not that it cuts any ice practically,' as he said. 'For good or ill, David was killed by the chandelier falling on him, and by no possible means could that verdict be shaken. Moreover, it would be a grave mistake to try and shake it now; the only result would be to upset Sir John and his sister, and lay oneself open to a severe rap on the knuckles for not having spoken at the time. But I'd give a lot, Bob, to know the truth about that night.'

'Well, you're never likely to, old man,' I answered, 'so I'd give up worrying.'

Which was where I went down to the bottom of the class; though even now the thing seems impossible. And yet it happened – happened the very evening I left. Ronald, who had stayed on, told me about it when he got back to London. Told me in short, clipped sentences with many pauses in between. Rarely have I seen him more savagely angry.

'I'm not a rich man, Bob, but I'd give ten thousand pounds to bring that swine to the gallows ... Who? ... Sir John Crawsham ... He murdered David and, but for the grace of God, he'd have got Michael ... There's only one thing to be said in his favour, if it can be regarded in that light; it was, I think, the cleverest scheme I have ever come across.

'We were all sitting in the hall after dinner last night, and the conversation turned on the secret passage. After a while, Sir John was prevailed on by Michael to go and get the paper on which the clues were supposed to be written, and Anne and Michael went into the music room and started to try to solve it. I was playing bridge and could not go with them, and I'd have liked to.

'Suddenly, I heard Michael give a shout of triumph, and by the mercy of Allah I was dummy. Otherwise—'

He bit at his pipe angrily.

'I got up and went to the door of the music room; Michael was standing in the right-hand inglenook, his hands on the panelling above his head, with Sir John beside him.

'"He's got it," cried Anne triumphantly, and there came a loud click. And then, Bob, number two solution flashed into my brain and I acted mechanically. I think some outside power made me move; I don't profess to say. I got to Michael, collared him round the knees and hurled him sideways, just as the panel slid open and out "something" whizzed over our heads.'

'Good God!' I muttered. 'What was it?'

'The most wickedly efficient death-trap I have ever seen. As the door opened, it operated a catch in the roof of the passage behind it. As soon as the catch was withdrawn, a jagged mass of iron weighing over sixty pounds was released, and, swinging like a pendulum on the end of a chain, hurtled through the opening at a height of about five feet from the ground. Anyone standing in the opening would have taken it in the lower part of the face, and literally been hit for six.

'We stood there white and shaking, watching the thing swing backwards and forwards. As it grew slower we were able to check it, and as it finally came to rest, the door shut. The room was normal again ...

'I won't bore you, Bob, with a description of the mechanism. That it was of great age was clear; it had been installed when the house was built. Anyway, that's not the interesting point; that began to come in on me gradually. I suppose I was a fool; one is at times. But for a while the blinding significance of the thing didn't strike me. Then suddenly I knew ... Involuntarily, I looked at Sir John; and he was staring at me ... For a second our eyes held; then he looked away ... But in that second he knew that I knew ...'

Ronald rose and helped himself to a drink.

'I may be dense,' I remarked, 'but I still don't quite see. It is clear that that is the thing that killed David, but even then there's no proof that Sir John was aware of it. From what you tell me, the door shut of its own accord.'

'As you say, that is the thing that killed David. As it killed that man forty years ago. And it lifted the body through the air with the force of the blow, and deposited it in the centre of the room. So much is obvious; the rest is surmise.

'Let us go back a little, Bob, and put a hypothetical case. And let us see how it fits in. A certain man – we will call him Robinson – was senior partner in a business. But though the senior, he drew but little more money from it than his two nephews. Which galled him.

'One day, Robinson happened to hear of a certain house – it is more than likely he got hold of some old document – which contained a very peculiar feature. It was for sale, and little by little a singularly devilish scheme began to mature in his mind. He studied it from every angle; he tested it link by link; and he found it perfect.

'He gave a housewarming party, where he enlarged upon an unsolved murder that had taken place years before. And late that night, after everyone else had gone to bed, he sat up with his elder nephew. After a while he turned the conversation to the secret passage, and they both went into the music room to look for it. Robinson, in spite of his statements to the contrary, knew, of course, where it was. And very skilfully, by a hint here and a hint there, he let his nephew discover it, as he thought, for himself. With the result we know.

'Had it failed, Robinson's whole plan would have failed. But no suspicion would have attached to him. He knew nothing about this infernal device. It did not fail; there in the centre of the floor was one of his partners dead. Robinson's third had become a half.

'Quietly he goes upstairs and gets into pyjamas. Then he cuts the rope of the chandelier. You see, the essence of his scheme was that the death trap should not be discovered; he wanted to use it just once more. For the whole is much better than a half. I've told you how he did it; fortunately without success.'

'But can't you go to the police, man?' I cried.

'What am I to say to 'em? What proof can I give them *now* that David was dead before the chandelier fell on him? Exhumation won't supply it; this isn't a poison case. I merely lay myself open to thundering damages for libel. Why, if I knew it, didn't I speak at the time?'

'How I wish you had!'

'Robinson would still have got off. Even if the chandelier hadn't killed David, it had fallen accidentally, and he knew nothing about the other thing.'

'I suppose it isn't possible that it *did* fall accidentally, and that Sir Job *did* know nothing about the other thing?'

Ronald gave a short laugh.

'Perfectly possible, if you will answer me one question. Who replaced the weight in position?'

How's Your Mother?

Simon Brett

'It's all right, Mother. Just the postman,' Humphrey Partridge called up the stairs, recognising the uniformed bulk behind the frosted glass of the front door.

'Parcel for you, Mr Partridge.' As he handed it over, Reg Carter the postman leant one arm against the doorframe in his chatting position. 'From some nurseries, it says on the label.'

'Yes—'

'Bulbs, by the feel of it.'

'Yes.' Humphrey Partridge's hand remained on the door, as if about to close it, but the postman didn't seem to notice the hint.

'Right time of year for planting bulbs, isn't it. November.'

'Yes.'

Again Reg was impervious to the curtness of the monosyllable. 'How's your mother?' he asked chattily.

Partridge softened. 'Not so bad. You know, considering.'

'Never seem to bring any letters for her, do I?'

'No. Well, when you get to that age, most of your friends have gone.'

'Suppose so. How old is she now?'

'Eighty-six last July.'

'That's a good age. Doesn't get about much.'

'No, hardly at all. Now if you'll excuse me, I do have to leave to catch my train.'

Humphrey Partridge just restrained himself from slamming the door on the postman. Then he put his scarf round his neck, crossed the ends across his chest and held them in position with his chin while he slipped on his raincoat with the fleecy lining buttoned in. He picked up his briefcase and called up the stairs, 'Bye bye, Mother. Off to work now. Be home usual time.'

In the village post office Mrs Denton watched the closing door with disapproval and shrugged her shawl righteously around her. 'Don't like that Jones woman. Coming in for *The Times* every morning. Very lah-di-dah. Seems shifty to me. Wouldn't be surprised if there was something going on there.'

'Maybe.' Her husband didn't look up from his morbid perusal of the *Daily Mirror*. 'Nasty business, this, about the woman and the RAF bloke.'

'The Red Scarf Case,' Mrs Denton italicised avidly.

'Hmm. They say when the body was found—' He broke off as Humphrey Partridge came in for his *Telegraph*. 'Morning. How's the old lady?'

'Oh, not too bad, thank you. Considering ...'

Mrs Denton gathered her arms under her bosom. 'Oh, Mr Partridge, the vicar was in yesterday, asked me if I'd ask you. There's a jumble sale in the Institute tomorrow and he was looking for some able-bodied helpers just to shift a few—'

'Ah, I'm sorry, Mrs Denton, I don't like to leave my mother at weekends. She's alone enough with me being at work all week.'

'It wouldn't be for long. It's just—'

'I'm sorry. Now I must dash or I'll miss my train.'

They let the silence stand for a moment after the shop door shut. Then Mr Denton spoke, without raising his eyes from his paper. 'Lives for his mother, that one.'

'Worse things to live for.'

'Oh yes. Still, doesn't seem natural in a grown man.'

'Shouldn't think it'd last long. Old girl must be on the way out. Been bedridden ever since they moved here. And how long ago's that? Three years?'

'Three. Four.'

'Don't know what he'll do when she goes.'

'Move maybe. George in the grocer's said something about him talking of emigrating to Canada if only he hadn't got the old girl to worry about.'

'I expect he'll come into some money when she goes.' When Mrs Denton expected something, it soon became fact in the village.

Humphrey Partridge straightened the ledgers on his desk, confident that the sales figures were all entered and his day's work was done. He stole a look at his watch. Five twenty-five. Nearly time to put his coat on and—

The phone rang. Damn. Why on earth did people ring up at such inconvenient times? 'Partridge,' he snapped into the receiver.

'Hello, it's Sylvia in Mr Brownlow's office. He wondered if you could just pop along for a quick word.'

'What, now? I was about to leave. Oh, very well, Miss Simpson. If it's urgent.'

Mr Brownlow looked up over his half-glasses as Partridge entered. 'Humphrey, take a pew.'

Partridge sat on the edge of the indicated chair, poised for speedy departure.

'Minor crisis blown up,' said Brownlow languidly. 'Know I was meant to be going to Antwerp next week, for the conference?'

'Yes.'

'Just had a telex from Parsons in Rome. Poor sod's gone down with some virus and is stuck in an Eyetie hospital, heaven help him. Means I'll have to go out to Rome tomorrow and pick up the pieces of the contract. So there's no chance of my making Antwerp on Monday.'

'Oh dear.'

'Yes, it's a bugger. But we've got to have someone out there. It's an important conference. Someone should be there waving the flag for Brownlow and Potter.'

'Surely Mr Potter will go.'

'No, he's too tied up here.'

'Evans?'

'On leave next week. Had it booked for yonks. No, Partridge, you're the only person who's free to go.'

'But I'm very busy this time of year.'

'Only routine. One of the juniors can keep it ticking over.'

'But surely it should be someone whose standing in the company—'

'Your standing's fine. Be good experience. About time you took some more executive responsibility. Bound to be a bit of a reshuffle when Potter retires and you're pretty senior on length of service ... Take that as read then, shall we? I'll get Sylvia to transfer the tickets and hotel and—'

'No, Mr Brownlow. You see, it's rather difficult.'

'What's the problem?'

'It's my mother. She's very old and I look after her, you know.'

'Oh come on, it's only three days, Partridge.'

'But she's very unwell at the moment.'

'She always seems to be very unwell.'

'Yes, but this time I think it's ... I mean I'd never forgive myself if ...'

'But this is important for the company. And Antwerp's not the end of the earth. I mean, if something happened, you could leap on to a plane and be back in a few hours.'

'I'm sorry. It's impossible. My mother ...'

Mr Brownlow sat back in his high swivel chair and toyed with a paper knife. 'You realise this would mean I'd have to send someone junior to you ...'

'Yes.'

'And it's the sort of thing that might stick in people's minds if there were a question of promotion or ...'

'Yes.'

'Yes. Well, that's it.' Those who knew Mr Brownlow well would have realised that he was extremely annoyed. 'I'd better not detain you any longer or I'll make you late for your train.'

Partridge looked gratefully at his watch as he rose. 'No, if I really rush, I'll just make it.'

'Oh, terrific,' said Mr Brownlow, but his sarcasm was wasted on Partridge's departing back.

'Mother, I'm home. Six thirty-five on the dot. Had to run for the train, but I just made it. I'll come on up.'

Humphrey Partridge bounded up the stairs, went past his own bedroom and stood in the doorway of the second bedroom. There was a smile of triumph on his lips as he looked at the empty bed.

Partridge put two slices of bread into his toaster. He had had the toaster a long time and it still worked perfectly. Better than one of those modern pop-up ones. Silly, gimmicky things.

He looked out of the kitchen window with satisfaction. He felt a bit stiff, but it had been worth it. The earth of the borders had all been neatly turned over. And all the bulbs planted. He smiled.

The doorbell rang. As he went to answer it, he looked at his watch. Hmm, have to get his skates on or he'd miss the train. Always more difficult to summon up the energy on Monday mornings.

It was Reg Carter the postman. 'Sorry, couldn't get these through the letterbox.' But there was no apology in his tone; no doubt he saw this as another opportunity for one of his interminable chats.

Partridge could recognise that the oversize package was more brochures and details about Canada. He would enjoy reading those on the train. He restrained the impulse to snatch them out of the postman's hand.

'Oh, and there was this letter too.'

'Thank you.'

Still the postman didn't hand them over. 'Nothing for the old lady today neither.'

'No, as I said last week, she doesn't expect many letters.'

'No. She all right, is she?'

'Fine, thank you.' The postman still seemed inclined to linger, so Partridge continued, I'm sorry. I'm in rather a hurry. I have to leave for work in a moment.'

The next thing Reg Carter knew, the package and letter were no longer in his hands and the door was shut in his face.

Inside Humphrey Partridge put the unopened brochures into his briefcase and slid his finger along the top of the other envelope. As he looked at its contents, he froze, then sat down at the foot of the stairs, weak with shock. Out loud he cried, 'This is it. Oh, Mother, this is it!'

Then he looked at his watch, gathered up his briefcase, scarf and coat, and hurried out of the house.

'There's more about the Red Scarf Case in the *Sun*,' said Mr Denton with gloomy relish.

'It all comes out at the trial. Always does,' his wife observed sagely.

'Says here he took her out on to the golf links to look at the moon. Look at the moon – huh!'

'I wouldn't be taken in by something like that, Maurice.

Serves her right in a way. Mind you, he must have been a psychopath. Sergeant Wallace says nine cases out of ten—'

Partridge entered breezily. '*Telegraph*, please. Oh, and a local paper, please.'

'Local paper?' Mrs Denton, starved of variety, pounced on this departure from the norm.

'Yes, I just want a list of local estate agents.'

'Thinking of buying somewhere else?'

'Maybe not buying,' said Partridge, coyly enigmatic.

He didn't volunteer any more, so Mr Denton took up the conversation with his habitual originality. 'Getting colder, isn't it?'

Partridge agreed that it was.

Mrs Denton added her contribution. 'It'll get a lot colder yet.'

'I'm sure it will,' Partridge agreed. And then he couldn't resist saying, 'Though with a bit of luck I won't be here to feel it.'

'You are thinking of moving then?'

'Maybe. Maybe.' And Humphrey Partridge left the shop with his newspapers, unwontedly frisky.

'I think,' pronounced Mrs Denton, focusing her malevolence, 'there's something going on there.'

'You wanted to see me, Partridge?'

'Yes, Mr Brownlow.'

'Well, make it snappy. I've just flown back from Rome. As it turns out I could have made the Antwerp conference. Still, it's giving young Dyett a chance to win his spurs. What was it you wanted, Partridge?' Mr Brownlow stifled a yawn.

'I've come to give in my notice.'

'You mean you want to leave?'

'Yes.'

'This is rather unexpected.'

'Yes, Mr Brownlow.'

'I see.' Mr Brownlow swivelled his chair in irritation. 'Have you had an offer from another company?'

'No.'

'No, I hardly thought ...'

'I'm going abroad. With my mother.'

'Of course. May one ask where?'

'Canada.'

'Ah. Reputed to be a land of opportunity. Are you starting a new career out there?'

'I don't know. I may not work.'

'Oh, come into money, have we?' But he received no answer to the question. 'OK, if you'd rather not say, that's your business. I won't enquire further. Well, I hope you know what you're doing. I'll need a month's notice in writing.'

'Is it possible for me to go sooner?'

'A month's notice is customary.' Mr Brownlow's temper suddenly gave. 'No, sod it, I don't want people here unwillingly. Just go. Go today!'

'Thank you.'

'Of course, we do usually give a farewell party to departing staff, but in your case ...'

'It won't be necessary.'

'Too bloody right it won't be necessary.' Mr Brownlow's eyes blazed. 'Get out!'

*

Partridge got home just before lunch in high spirits. Shamelessly using Brownlow and Potter's telephones for private calls, he had rung an estate agent to put his house on the market and made positive enquiries of the Canadian High Commission about emigration. He burst through the front door and called out his customary, 'Hello, Mother. I'm home.'

The words died on his lips as he saw Reg Carter emerging from his kitchen. 'Good God, what are you doing here? This is private property.'

'I was doing my rounds with the second post.'

'How did you get in?'

'I had to break a window.'

'You had no right. That's breaking and entering. I'll call the police.'

'It's all right. I've already called them. I've explained it all to Sergeant Wallace.'

Partridge's face was the colour of putty. 'Explained what?' he croaked.

'About the fire.' Then again, patiently, because Partridge didn't seem to be taking it in. 'The fire. There was a fire. In your kitchen. I saw the smoke as I came past. You'd left the toaster on this morning. It had got the tea towel and the curtains were just beginning to go. So I broke in.'

Partridge now looked human again. 'I understand. I'm sorry I was so suspicious. It's just ... Thank you.'

'Don't mention it,' said Reg Carter with insouciance he'd learned from some television hero. 'It was just I thought, what with your mother upstairs, I couldn't afford to wait and call the fire brigade. What with her not being able to move and all.'

'That was very thoughtful. Thank you.' Unconsciously Partridge was edging round the hall, as if trying to usher the postman out. But Reg Carter stayed firmly in the kitchen doorway. Partridge reached vaguely towards his wallet. I feel I should reward you in some way ...'

'No, I don't want no reward. I just did it to save the old lady.'

Partridge gave a little smile and nervous nod of gratitude.

'I mean, it would be awful for her to be trapped. Someone helpless like that.'

'Yes.'

Up until this point the postman's tone had been tentative, but, as he continued, he became more forceful. 'After I'd put the fire out, I thought I ought to see if she was all right. She might have smelt burning or heard me breaking in and been scared out of her wits ... So I called up the stairs to her. She didn't answer.'

The colour was once again dying rapidly from Partridge's face. 'No, she's very deaf. She wouldn't hear you.'

'No. So I went upstairs,' Reg Carter continued inexorably. 'All the doors were closed. I opened one. I reckon it must be your room. Then I opened another. There was a bed there. But there was no one in it.'

'No.'

'There was no one in the bathroom. Or anywhere. The house was empty.'

'Yes.'

The postman looked for a moment at his quarry, then said, 'I thought that was rather strange, Mr Partridge. I mean, you told us all your mother was bedridden and lived here.'

'She does — I mean she did.' The colour was back in his cheeks in angry blushes.

'Did?'

'Yes, she died,' said Partridge quickly.

'Died? When? You said this morning when I asked after her that—'

'She died a couple of days ago. I'm sorry, I've been in such a state. The shock, you know. You can't believe that it's happened and—'

'When was the funeral?'

A new light of confusion came into Partridge's eyes as he stumbled to answer. 'Yesterday. Very recently. It's only just happened. I'm sorry, I'm not thinking straight. I don't know whether I'm coming or going.'

'No.' Reg Carter's voice was studiously devoid of intonation. I'd better be on my way. Got a couple more letters to deliver, then back to the post office.'

Humphrey Partridge mumbled more thanks as he ushered the postman out of the front door. When he heard the click of the front gate, he sank trembling on to the bottom stair and cried out loud, 'Why, why can't they leave us alone?'

Sergeant Wallace was a fat man with a thin, tidy mind. He liked everything in its place and he liked to put it there himself. The one thing that frightened him was the idea of anyone else being brought in to what he regarded as his area of authority, in other words, anything that happened in the village. So it was natural for him, when the rumours about Humphrey Partridge reached unmanageable proportions, to go and see the man himself rather than reporting to his superiors.

It was about a week after the fire. Needless to say, Reg Carter had talked to Mr and Mrs Denton and they had talked to practically everyone who came into the post office. The talk was now so wild that something had to be done.

Humphrey Partridge opened his front door with customary lack of welcome, but Sergeant Wallace forced his large bulk inside, saying he'd come to talk about the fire.

Tea chests in the sitting room told their own story. 'Packing your books I see, Mr Partridge.'

'Yes. Most of my effects will be going to Canada by sea.' Partridge assumed, rightly, that the entire village knew of his impending departure.

'When is it exactly you're off?'

'About a month. I'm not exactly sure.'

Sergeant Wallace settled his uninvited mass into an armchair. 'Nice place, Canada, I hear. My nephew's over there.'

'Ah.'

'You'll be buying a place to live …?'

'Yes.'

'On your own.'

'Yes.'

'Your mother's no longer with you?'

'No. She … she died.'

'Yes. Quite recently, I hear.' Sergeant Wallace stretched out, as if warming himself in front of the empty grate. 'It was to some extent about your mother that I called.'

Partridge didn't react, so the sergeant continued. 'As you know, this is a small place and most people take an interest in other people's affairs …'

'Can't mind their own bloody business, most of them.'

'Maybe so. Now I don't listen to gossip, but I do have to keep my ear to the ground – that's what the job's about. And I'm afraid I've been hearing some strange things about you recently, Mr Partridge.'

Sergeant Wallace luxuriated in another pause. 'People are saying things about your mother's death. I realise, being so recent, you'd probably rather not talk about it.'

'Fat chance I have of that. Already I'm getting anonymous letters and phone calls about it.'

'And you haven't reported them?'

'Look, I'll be away soon. And none of it will matter.'

'Hmm.' The sergeant decided the moment had come to take the bull by the horns. 'As you'll probably know from these letters and telephone calls then, people are saying you killed your mother for her money.'

'That is libellous nonsense!'

'Maybe. I hope so. If you can just answer a couple of questions for me, then I'll know so. Tell me first, when did your mother die?'

'Ten days ago. The eleventh.'

'Are you sure? It was on the eleventh that you had the fire and Reg Carter found the house empty.'

'I'm sorry. A couple of days before that. It's been such a shock, I ...'

'Of course.' Sergeant Wallace nodded soothingly. 'And so the funeral must have been on the tenth?'

'Some time round then, yes.'

'Strange that none of the local undertakers had a call from you.'

'I used a firm from town, one I have connections with.'

'I see.' Sergeant Wallace looked rosier than ever as he warmed to his task. 'And no doubt it was a doctor from town who issued the death certificate?'

'Yes.'

'Do you happen to have a copy of that certificate?' the sergeant asked sweetly.

Humphrey Partridge looked weakly at his tormentor and murmured, 'You know I don't.'

'If there isn't a death certificate,' mused Sergeant Wallace agonisingly slowly, 'then that suggests there might be something unusual about your mother's death.'

'Damn you! Damn you all!' Partridge was almost sobbing with passion. 'Why can't you leave me alone? Why are you always prying?'

The sergeant recovered from his surprise. 'Mr Partridge, if a crime's been committed—'

'No crime's been committed!' Partridge shouted in desperate exasperation. 'I haven't got a mother. I never saw my mother. She walked out on me when I was six months old and I was brought up in care.'

'Then who was living upstairs?' asked Sergeant Wallace logically.

'Nobody. I live on my own, I always have lived on my own. Don't you see, I hate people.' The confession was costing Partridge a lot, but he was too wound up to stop its outpouring. 'People are always trying to find out about you, to probe, to know you. They want to invade your house, take you out for drinks, invade your privacy. I can't stand it. I just want to be on my own!'

Sergeant Wallace tried to interject, but Partridge

steamrollered on. 'But you can't be alone. People won't let you. You have to have a reason. So I invented my mother. I couldn't do things, I couldn't see people, because I had to get back to my mother. She was ill. And my life worked very well like that. I even began to believe in her, to talk to her. She never asked questions, she didn't want to know anything about me, she just loved me and was kind and beautiful. And I loved her. I wouldn't kill her – I wouldn't lay a finger on her – it's you, all of you who've killed her!' He was now weeping uncontrollably. 'Damn you, damn you.'

Sergeant Wallace took a moment or two to organise this new information in his mind. 'So what you're telling me is, there never was any mother. You made her up. You couldn't have killed her, because she never lived.'

'Yes,' said Partridge petulantly. 'Can't you get that through your thick skull?'

'Hmm. And how do you explain that you suddenly have enough money to emigrate and buy property in Canada?'

'My premium bond came up. I got the letter on the morning of the fire. That's why I forgot to turn the toaster off. I was so excited.'

'I see.' Sergeant Wallace lifted himself ponderously out of his chair and moved across to the window. 'Been digging in the garden, I see.'

'Yes, I put some bulbs in.'

'Bulbs, and you're about to move.' The sergeant looked at his quarry. 'That's very public-spirited of you, Mr Partridge.'

The post office was delighted with the news of Partridge's arrest. Mrs Denton was firmly of the opinion that she had thought there was something funny going on and recognised Partridge's homicidal tendencies. Reg Carter bathed in the limelight of having set the investigation in motion and Sergeant Wallace, though he regretted the intrusion of the CID into his patch, felt a certain satisfaction for his vital groundwork.

The Dentons were certain Reg would be called as a witness at the trial and thought there was a strong possibility that they might be called as character witnesses. Mrs Denton bitterly regretted the demise of the death penalty, feeling that prison was too good for people who strangled old ladies in their beds. Every passing shopper brought news of the developments in the case, how the police had dug up the garden, how they had taken up the floorboards, how they had been heard tapping the walls of Partridge's house. Mrs Denton recommended that they should sift through the ashes of the boiler.

So great was the community interest in the murder that the cries of disbelief and disappointment were huge when the news came through that the charges against Partridge had been dropped. The people of the village felt that they had been robbed of a pleasure which, by any scale of values, was rightfully theirs.

But as the details seeped out, it was understood that Partridge's wild tale to Sergeant Wallace was true. There had been no one else living in the house. He had had a large premium bond win. And the last record of Partridge's real mother dated from four years previously when she had been found guilty of soliciting in Liverpool and sentenced to two months in prison.

The village's brief starring role in the national press was over and its people, disgruntled and cheated, returned to more domestic scandals. Humphrey Partridge came back to his house, but no one saw him much as he hurried to catch up on the delay to his emigration plans which his wrongful arrest had caused him.

It was two days before his departure, in the early evening, when he had the visitor. It was December, dark and cold. Everyone in the village was indoors.

He did not recognise the woman standing on the doorstep. She was dressed in a short black and white fun-fur coat, which might have been fashionable five years before. Her hair was fierce ginger, a strident contrast to scarlet lipstick, and black lashes hovered over her eyes like bats' wings. The stringiness of her neck and the irregular bumps of veins under her black stockings denied the evidence of her youthful dress.

'Hello, Humphrey,' she said.

'Who are you?' He held the door, as usual, ready to close it.

The woman laughed, a short, unpleasant sound. 'No, I don't expect you to recognise me. You were a bit small when we last met.'

'You're not ...?'

'Yes, of course I am. Aren't you going to give your mother a kiss?'

She thrust forward her painted face and Partridge recoiled back into the hall. The woman took the opportunity to follow him in and shut the front door behind her.

'Nice little place you've got for yourself, Humphrey.' She advanced and Partridge backed away from her into the sitting room. She took in the bareness and the packing cases. 'Oh yes, of course, leaving these shores, aren't you? I read in the paper. Canada, was it? Nice people, Canadians. At least, their sailors are.' Another burst of raucous laughter.

''Cause of course you've got the money now, haven't you, Humphrey? I read about that too. Funny, I never met anyone before what'd won a premium bond. Plenty who did all right on the horses, but not premium bonds.'

'What do you want?' Partridge croaked.

'Just come to see my little boy, haven't I? Just thinking, now you're set up so nice and cosy, maybe you ought to help your mum in her old age.'

'I don't owe you anything. You never did anything for me. You walked out on me.'

'Ah, that was ages ago. And he was a nice boy, Clinton. I had to have a fling. I meant to come back to you after a week or two. But then the council moved in and Clinton got moved away and—'

'What do you want?'

'I told you. I want to be looked after in my old age. I read in the paper about how devoted you were to your old mother.' Again the laugh.

'But you aren't my mother.' Partridge was speaking with great care and restraint.

'Oh yes, I am, Humphrey.'

'You're not.'

'Yes. Ooh, I've had a thought – why don't you take your old mother to Canada with you?'

'You are not my mother!' Partridge's hands were on the woman's shoulders, shaking out the emphasis of his words.

'I'm your mother, Humphrey.'

His hands rose to her neck to silence the taunting words. They tightened and shuddered as he spoke. 'My mother is beautiful and kind. She is nothing like you. She always loved me. She still loves me!'

The spasm passed. He released his grip. The woman's body slipped down. As her head rolled back, her false teeth fell out with a clatter on to the floor.

Sergeant Wallace appeared to be very busy with a ledger when Humphrey Partridge went into the police station next morning. He was embarrassed by what had happened. It didn't fit inside the neat borders of his mind and it made him look inefficient. But eventually he could pretend to be busy no longer. 'Good morning, Mr Partridge. What can I do for you?'

'I leave for Canada tomorrow.'

'Oh. Well, may I wish you every good fortune in your new life there.'

'Thank you.' A meagre smile was on Partridge's lips. 'Sergeant, about my mother ...'

Sergeant Wallace closed his ledger with some force. 'Listen Mr Partridge, you have already had a full apology and—'

'No, no, it's nothing to do with that. I just wanted to tell you ...'

'Yes?'

'... that I *did* kill my mother.'

'Oh yes, and then I suppose you buried her in the garden, eh?'

'Yes, I did.'

'Fine.' Sergeant Wallace reopened his ledger and looked down at the page busily.

'I'm confessing to murder,' Partridge insisted.

The sergeant looked up with an exasperated sigh. 'Listen, Mr Partridge, I'm very sorry about what happened and you're entitled to your little joke, but I do have other things to do, so, if you wouldn't mind ...'

'You mean I can just go?'

'Please.'

'To Canada?'

'To where you bloody well like.'

'Right then, I'll go. And ... er ... leave the old folks at home.'

Sergeant Wallace didn't look up from his ledger as Partridge left the police station.

Outside, Humphrey Partridge took a deep breath of air, smiled and said out loud, 'Right, Mother, Canada it is.'

Credits